dark before dawn

Editor
Andy Cox

Publisher & UK Office
TTA Press, 5 Martins Lane, Witcham,
Ely, Cambs CB6 2LB
t: 01353 777931
e: ttapress@aol.com

USA Office
Wayne Edwards, TTA Press, PO Box 219,
Olyphant, PA 18447
e: we21011@earthlink.net

w: www.tta-press.freewire.co.uk

Four-Issue Subscriptions
UK £22 • Europe £26 • RoW £30 • USA $40

Submissions
Unsolicited submissions of short stories
welcome. Please study several issues of
Crimewave before submitting and always
enclose a brief covering letter and a self-
addressed stamped envelope. Overseas
submissions should be disposable and
accompanied by two IRCs or simply an
email address (this option is for overseas
submissions only). Writers from North
America can send their stories to the USA
office (SAE essential). Send only one story
at a time, preferably mailed flat or folded
no more than once. Do not send submissions by recorded delivery. There is no
length restriction placed on the stories
published in Crimewave, but we don't
accept reprints or simultaneous submissions. Letters and queries are very
welcome via email but unsolicited story
submissions are not – they will simply be
deleted. No responsibility can be accepted
for loss or damage to unsolicited material,
howsoever caused

ISSN
1463 1350

ISBN
0 9526947 5 1

CONTENTS

5

The Mojave is a graveyard. It lies between Los Angeles and Las Vegas, and through it runs a road where, in the middle of desert nights, all of the human predators in those two cities come to dump their prey. Boys and girls, tied up in the trunk, scared and bleeding in the back seat, already dead in a cheap plastic bag. Often, they don't even bother to bury them. They simply drag them far enough away from the road that a passing car won't spot them. Sometimes they do bury them, shallowly in the dry earth. If all of the dead people stood up at once, the desert would be as full as the cities that lie on its edges. Besides the dead, the desert is a burying ground for nuclear waste, for garbage and slag from the silver and gold mines, for abandoned cars and for abandoned people. Outcasts huddle in shacks far out in the night, away from prying eyes. In makeshift labs they mix methamphetamine and speed. Everything discarded, everything killed or broken or un-wanted, it seems, ends up here. Sometimes, people find things. A hiker stumbles across a skull, a rusted six-shooter, a dead cowboy who took shade under a Joshua tree a hundred years ago and never moved again. The police dig up a body and find two more beneath it. Most of the time, though, things stay buried . . .

Dark, dangerous, and intoxicating, Ray Nayler's fiction is a potent elixir that will slam your senses. It will leave you shaken and stirred, with cool characters on ice, and a plot served up neat with a twist. Ready for a heady shot and a slow burn?' **Elise Lyons, Blue Murder**

Ray Nayler's crime fiction claws its way into your mind and won't leave. He writes like Jim Thompson on crack, only his prose is better!' **Anthony Neil Smith, Plots With Guns**

The first Crimewave Special is a novel by Ray Nayler, whose story 'Cutting Wood, Carrying Water' appeared in Crimewave 4. American Graveyards is in the same format as the regular Crimewave, with another astonishing night-time photograph by Troy Paiva on the cover. Less ethical publishers would make you pay a small fortune for this collectors' item, but we're only charging the same as a normal issue of Crimewave. Simply send a cheque for £6 (£7 Europe, £8 RoW, $12 USA), payable to TTA Press, to either of our UK or USA offices (see page 4 for addresses) NB: Crimewave Specials do not form part of your subscription

american graveyards

a kick in the lunchbucket
sean doolittle

Sean Doolittle's short fiction has been published in a variety of magazines and anthologies, and this is his second appearance in Crimewave. His first novel, Dirt, a crime thriller set in and around a crooked funeral home, is out now from US publisher UglyTown (www. UglyTown.com/Dirt). Sean lives in the middle of the American midwest with his wife Jessica and daughter Kate.

I'm one of the world's great watchers.

The attractive young woman sitting on a park bench, looking at her wristwatch and smoothing her skirt. Two twelve year-olds pow-wowing by a magazine rack about which one tries to buy the smokes this time. A guy in a horrible toupee thumping cantaloupes at the supermarket; the skateboarders landing moves on the steps in front of the city library. A big burly bear of a man and a slight soft whisper of a woman, holding hands and eating ice cream from the same paper cup.

I could sit and watch for hours. A friend once suggested I was inherently nosy, end of story. My girlfriend says I do it because I get bored with my own life too easily. It's neither of these, or possibly both, but why analyze it to death? It's just the way I've always been: the kind of guy who loves a good mall on a Saturday.

Personally, I've always liked to believe that there's a certain level of artistry involved. Make eye contact with the wrong sort of person, you could wind up with an ugly moment on your hands. Bumble your way into convincing some Gold's Gym hothead you're staring at his date? You've just poured yourself a glass of fire, my friend. Or worse: intrude obviously — unforgivably — on someone in genuine pain. See how that makes you feel.

Watching is an art form. An underlying philosophy is fine — but to do it right, tactical skills are what you really need.

Learn how to divert your gaze. Make those sunglasses work for you. One of my own favorites: using reflections. I once watched, for twenty thrilling minutes or more, the inverted projection of two women in black leather jackets soul kissing in the film of antifreeze on a water puddle near a curb after a late-afternoon rain.

I'm one of the world's great watchers. And I can always spot an amateur.

So the first night I noticed the guy in the rusted Ford Tempo parked across our street, I craved backstory. I wondered what he was doing there, slouched in the dark behind the wheel. I wondered why he was watching the neighbor's house through a pair of compact field binoculars.

I wondered if I should call a cop. Or mind my own business. Or at least wander next door and give a neighborly heads-up.

I considered all of that. Of course I did.

But my very first thought about the guy in the car was *fella, you've got a lot to learn.*

The second night, I called Erin over.

"Check it out. There he is out there again."

"There who is out where again?"

"The *guy*. With the binocs. I told you all about him."

"Oh." Erin emerged from the bathroom buttoning a lacy black shirt over the slender silver navel ring she'd recently begun wearing again. "So what's he doing?"

"Scoping out next door, same as last night. Look at him!" Through the narrow gap in the living room drapes, I said: "Psst. Hey, dumbass. Everybody can see you."

Erin joined me at the window, smelling faintly of the lavender body wash I'd given her on Valentine's Day. "I don't see anybody."

"Across the street. That crappy white Ford."

"Mm." She leaned over my shoulder and peered. "How can you see anything? It's totally dark."

"Just watch. He's there."

She gave it another beat and marked him. "Who, that guy?"

"That's him."

"He's just sitting there."

"Wait."

We waited. The guy behind the wheel of the car didn't move. He looked like he could have been sleeping.

After a minute, Erin finally sighed. "I should've known this would happen."

"What?"

"You."

I told her I didn't know what she was talking about; she rolled her eyes. I leaned over and gave her a kiss on the neck. She really did smell great. "Going out?"

"Amy wants to meet for drinks."

"Again?"

"Yes, love. Again." I could read her expression. *Ease up*, it said. "I told you she and Darrin are having a rough time."

"Tell her to float that guy already. He's a lunatic."

"Please. He isn't either."

"Oh, no?" I looked at her. "The guy goes around quoting professional wrestlers, Erin. He collects dummy hand grenades from Army surplus stores because he thinks they make 'bitchin' knacks.' His exact words."

"That's enough."

"Last year, when he had the band over for the Holyfield fight? Remember?"

"I remember."

"He tried to sell us Amway! Paul had to fake stomach cramps just to get us out of there. And it was only the second round."

Erin was looking at me severely — but I could tell she was trying not to smile. "Everybody has interests."

"Interests," I said. "Darrin Varga's got interests, all right. The guy bought a three-thousand dollar computer system just so he could download porn. He told me."

"Look, I didn't say he was a neurosurgeon. But Amy loves him, so cut the girl a little slack, will you please? She's miserable."

"Hey. Do I judge?"

"Oh, never."

I reached around, ran a hand up underneath her shirt, and let it rest in the warm smooth small of her back. When I went to kiss her on the mouth, she slipped me. "Make-up."

"Oops." I leaned back and looked her over, brushed the fabric of her shirt. "Have I seen this one before?"

"Nope. I just bought it this afternoon." She struck a pose. "Like it?"

"Extremely sexy," I told her, moving the drape an inch wider and glancing out the window. "There he goes again! I can't believe this guy."

As I turned, Erin stepped back to make room. At first I assumed she was watching along. But then I could sense her smirking behind me.

"I swear to god, sweetie, you really need to get a life."

"And miss this?"

Erin watched me watch for a moment more, then drew a parting breath. "Okay.

I'm off to play therapist. Don't wait up."

"Mm." I looked out the window. "Have a nice time."

"Oh, you too."

THE THIRD NIGHT, I FINALLY DECIDED TO STOP WATCHING. I MEAN, ENOUGH WAS enough. This was getting ridiculous.

"Hey."

At first, the guy tried to ignore me. He really was hopeless.

"Hey." I rapped on his window with my knuckle. "Roll it down, Sneaky Pete. I want to talk to you."

It was ten-thirty, dark, but the dope had parked right beneath a streetlamp. In the amber light, I could see him through the glass. He looked about my age, maybe mid-thirties. He had a wide meaty face and a dark ball cap pulled down over round bleary eyes. He kept pretending to read a newspaper, as if he hadn't even noticed I was there. But then he gave up, looked over, and made a sharp sweeping motion with his hand. *Shoo.*

We met gazes only momentarily. I'd already used my planned material and was somewhat at a loss in terms of next moves. So I let instinct lead and leaned down close to the glass. Cupping my hands around my mouth, I shouted, "Stop spying on my neighbors!"

And before the echo of the words rang away down the vacant street, the stranger's expression bloomed — from annoyance to open exasperation, finally flowering into horror.

He flung the newspaper away; when the thin pages fanned uncooperatively, he pummeled them into the passenger seat with his fist. Then he was groping for the keys in the ignition. Gaze locked front and center, the stranger cranked the engine.

And with a shudder, a tire scratch, and a belch of thick blue exhaust, he dropped the car into gear and tore away from the curb.

The last I saw of the guy, he was clipping a garbage can on the corner as he hung a hard right, bounced two wheels up over the curb, and lurched away down the intersecting street like a failed driver's exam.

"DO YOU REALLY WANT MY OPINION?"

"Of course I do."

Without looking up from the morning paper, Erin said, "I think you should just try not obsessing about it."

"Who's obsessing? I just think it's strange as hell." I used the spatula to push half the scrambled eggs onto Erin's plate and kept the rest. She reached for her fork, still reading. I leaned against the counter and ate from the pan. "You're telling me you don't think it's slightly weird?"

"The whole world's weird, Scott."

"Yeah, but this is like right-in-your-own-neighborhood weird."

"It's barely even our neighborhood yet," she said. "How do you know? Maybe this is normal for around here."

"Some help you are."

We'd only moved into the house last weekend — a sweaty and disorganized operation that ended up taking two days and several snippy exchanges longer than planned. But we were in.

These new digs of ours were an overdue upgrade from the cramped studio apartment we'd shared downtown for a little over a year. I don't think either of us had quite adjusted yet to the whole idea of yard implements and power tools. But it was a great place, loaded with character — one of those sunny story-and-a-half bungalows in a quirky older residential area, the kind of neighborhood that used to be suburbs before the city sprawled beyond on all sides, ring by concentric ring of business parks and strip malls and upmarket planned communities.

As Erin headed out the front door on her way to work, I said, "So you don't think I should go over there and tell them they're under surveillance?"

She planted a quick one on the corner of my mouth and patted me on the cheek. "Whatever makes you feel better, babe. Just do me one favor?"

"Sure."

"Unpack a box first, okay?"

WHAT I DID WAS WANDER THE QUIET HOUSE FOR AWHILE, EXPLORING OVERLOOKED nooks and unnoticed crannies. It's always been one of my favorite things about moving into a new place: those first few days discovering the cracks and corners of your new world. And it's one of my favorite things about making a living as a freelance graphic artist: the freedom to putter around your new place in a robe and sweatpants while regular people sit in morning traffic on their way to the office, or the cash register, or wherever they'll be spending their day in exchange for a wage.

I found just the right spot for Erin's grandmother's violin chair, a good place to nail up a picture ledge. I found an electrical knob that didn't appear to do anything. I found four stacks of spare bathroom tiles in the basement under the stairs.

In the process, I managed to burn through a half dozen unpacked boxes. By noon, I was pooped and hungry. So I threw on some jeans and walked to the gyro place I'd noticed a few blocks up on the main commercial street nearest us.

It was a gorgeous spring day, sunny and fragrant. On the walk, I let myself smoke a rare cigarette and relished every drag. The restaurant turned out to be everything I'd been hoping it would be: a small, boisterous place, dense with rich clinging Mediterranean smells, with greasy air and an open counter and a great swarthy guy in a dirty apron taking orders in English and singing them back over his shoulder in Greek.

I got a salad with feta and a sandwich with everything. By the time I slid into a corner booth with my tray, I was in one of those vibrant, good-natured, no-particular-reason moods.

So when my booth quaked under the sudden weight of someone uninvited depositing themselves across from me, I looked up with a mouthful of lamb enjoying the peculiar surprise.

But when I saw who it was, something cold slipped through my bowels. It was a queasy, caught sensation.

One of the facilities attendant to being one of the world's great watchers is that I never seem to forget a face. And I recognized his immediately, even without the ball cap.

"I don't know why *you* look so nervous," he told me. "You're the one who wanted to talk to me so bad."

For a numb vacant minute, I just sat, aware of the onion strand hanging idiotically from my lips, wondering how to handle this worrisome situation that had developed in my booth while I wasn't looking. Chewing, I bought another few moments by folding the edges of the foil wrapper around the remains of my sandwich; placing it in its basket; using my napkin to wipe cucumber sauce from my chin.

"Listen," I finally said, keeping my voice low. "I don't want any trouble."

When I'd first walked in, I'd noticed three uniformed cops having lunch in a booth against the far wall. I tried to take comfort in the idea that if this moon-faced lummox came over the table at me, at least one of them probably had a baton.

"So you just decided this now I guess?"

"I . . . I'm sorry," I said. "I don't know what you mean."

"I mean if I was trouble, seems like you already could've wound up with plenty of it," he said. He reached across the table and snatched a French fry out of my basket, using it as a gesturing tool before feeding it into his lantern-jawed mug. "Last night, I mean. Guess it's lucky for you I'm not trouble, huh?"

"I . . . " I stopped and actually thought about it. "I guess it is."

He took another fry and made it disappear. In the light of day, at shared-booth distance, the guy seemed older than I'd originally made him out to be. Mostly it was the thinning hair, which sort of hovered above his wide flat scalp in fine sandy wisps.

But the face itself did seem younger than the overall package suggested. Broad and thick, lightly pitted in spots by acne scars, but a young man's face. His eyes, which I remembered only half-lidded, turned out to be oddly striking. They were set wide, clear pale blue — a pair of bright pastel headlamps seated beneath a prominent slab of a brow. He wore a thin, out-of-style sport jacket that strained at the shoulders; his sleeve receded to mid-forearm when he reached across the table for another fry.

"How about I just go ahead and answer your first three questions so we can save a little time," he said. "Yes, I followed you here. No, I'm not dangerous. Yes, I plan to keep eating your fries."

"Um . . . okaay." I narrowed my eyes. "Question four?"

"Shoot."

"Why?"

He looked at me oddly, then shrugged. "I didn't think I was hungry, but they smelled good."

"I mean why are you following me?"

He seemed about to answer when one of the cops, toting a stack of empty baskets, glanced over at us on his way to the garbage can. When the cop saw my new lunch companion, he grinned, tilted back his head in greeting, and said: "Now there's a misdemeanor waiting to happen."

"Hey there, Ray. What's the news?"

"Nothing worth printing in a family paper."

"Tell me about it."

The cop dumped his empties and swung by our booth. His expression was pleasant, his tone conversational. "So you staying out of trouble, or what's the deal?"

"Whenever it's a slow week."

Officer Ray smirked. He looked at me. "Word of advice? Keep an eye on this guy."

"Oh, don't worry," said the stranger in my booth. "He is."

Officer Ray laughed and clapped him on one stout shoulder. "Okay. You take it easy."

"Same to you, Ray. Give Angie a hug for me."

"Will do."

By this point, my unease had eroded into a vast open sinkhole of curiosity. The guy watched me patiently, eating French fries, while I watched the cop return to his lunchmates.

And when Officer Ray was beyond earshot, the stranger returned to my original question as though rewinding a tape. I actually had to scramble a moment to remember what we'd been talking about.

"Following people is my business," he said. He reached inside the sport coat and produced a small leather business card carrier. "That's what it generally boils down to, anyway."

I took the rectangle he'd extended between thick-knuckled fingers. His card was simple and direct, plain black type on basic white cardstock: JACK DOPPLER – DISCREET PRIVATE INVESTIGATIONS. There was a phone number and a PO box printed below. Centered in between the lines of text was a small logo, which had been printed so badly that at first I thought it was a smudge. But after looking closer, I identified the image: an unblinking eye.

"Doppler," I commented. "Just like the radar." For some reason, I'd automatically begun trying to keep my tone cool and quippy, like his. But internally, I was sizzling with interest. A private investigator!

"Gee," he said wearily, munching down another one of my fries. "I've never heard that one before."

This was cooler than anything I could think of. I offered him back his card, but he was already putting away his carrier, so I dropped the card into my shirt pocket and looked at him. I wondered if he carried a handgun.

"Scott Brady," I told him, extending my hand.

"I know. I looked at your mail."

"You what?"

"I said I checked your mail. This morning. Before you came out to get it."

Retracting my hand, I thought: *is he serious?* This big snoopy bastard had actually walked up to our door and pawed through the contents of our mailbox? *While* I was home?

How awesome was that?

I moved my basket toward the center of the table so he wouldn't have to reach so far.

"So what's this about?" I said. "Are you on some kind of case or something?"

"Something," Jack Doppler said.

"You're tailing my neighbor?"

He looked at me and sighed.

I picked up my sandwich and began to unwrap it again. "So what's going on, anyway? Insurance thing? Some guy cheating on his wife?" I took a big bite and talked around it, surreptitiously eyeing the beleaguered seams of Jack Doppler's sport jacket to see if I could detect the outline of a shoulder holster. "Some wife cheating on her husband?"

"I'm not able to discuss the details of the case," he said simply.

The objective part of me was equal parts fascinated, amused, and dismayed by the magic a few minutes and one cheap business card could work on my viewpoint. All of a sudden, the guy didn't appear so much luggish and balding as he did cagey and hard-wearing. Vibe-wise, he'd morphed from Randy Quaid to Harvey Keitel practically right in front of my eyes.

"Oh. Right. Sure." I took another bite of my sandwich. "Can I ask you another question?"

He didn't say no.

"Actually, it's sort of the same question again," I said. "Where do I fit in?"

"You don't," he said. "That's exactly the point."

"I don't understand."

"No kidding." Jack Doppler looked at me for a long moment. He glanced over and lifted his chin toward Officer Ray and the other two cops as they made their way out the front door.

Then he took a napkin from my little stack and wiped French fry grease from his fingertips. "You want to know why I followed you? Truthfully?"

"Well . . . yeah."

"I don't know," he admitted, and suddenly his voice gained an exhausted undertone. "Let's just say it's been a frustrating week and I'm very, very tired. Last night, I'll come right out and tell you, you didn't do me any favors."

"Oh."

"Seeing you squirm for a minute or two seemed like it might be therapeutic." He shrugged. "Wasn't really. And it's unprofessional. I apologize."

"Oh." I didn't really know what to else to say. "No problem."

We sat there for a silent moment. Finally Jack Doppler spoke again. "As long as I'm here, would *you* mind answering a question for *me*?"

"I can try."

"Did you happen to mention anything to your neighbor about last night?"

"No."

He nodded. "Any plans along those lines?"

"I honestly hadn't decided yet," I said.

"Fair enough." Doppler tapped a rhythm on the tabletop with his thumbs. "Mind if I ask you a favor?"

"Decide not to?"

"If it wouldn't be too much trouble," he said.

I looked at him. He looked at me.

"Look," Doppler said. "All I can tell you is that this thing I'm working on means a great deal to the family who hired me. If you could just help me out here, you'd be helping ease some very real worry for some very decent folks."

I pondered what was left of my fries.

"Assuming," Doppler added, "my cover isn't already completely blown."

At this, I looked up. I couldn't help it. "Would it be okay with you if I made an observation?"

He regarded me curiously. "Feel free."

"Okay, don't get me wrong. I mean I'm sure you know what you're doing. And it's not like I'm some kind of expert, but . . . "

"Yeah?" Jack Doppler said.

I winced internally and forged on. "Look, forgive me for saying so, but your cover didn't exactly seem all that *deep*, you know? I mean even my girlfriend had you made. And she's basically oblivious."

Doppler leaned back an inch or two and folded his arms. He appraised me openly, without comment. I tried to read his face, but nothing showed there. His blue eyes remained clear. One corner of his mouth turned up briefly — but it wasn't quite a smirk, not quite a smile. Only movement.

"You're right," he finally said. "You're no expert."

I shrugged amiably.

"But I'll let you in on a professional secret," he added. "Most people don't suspect anybody's watching."

I thought about this for a second. I looked back across the table at Jack Doppler, PI. "No?"

And now a certain light did glint somewhere in those pale blue eyes.

"Hey," Jack Doppler said. "I followed you here, didn't I?"

I'M STILL NOT CERTAIN WHEN IT OCCURRED TO ME, OR WHY I ACTUALLY DECIDED to come out with it. Maybe I felt bad. Or maybe I was just doing what Erin tells me I have a sad habit of doing, unconsciously seeking the approval of anybody who strikes me as exotic or interesting.

Or maybe I was just so hopelessly intrigued by the idea of secrets and stakeouts and real-life private eye stuff in my very own neighborhood that I couldn't bear to let it all go away so soon.

Whatever the reason, when Jack Doppler tugged at his cuff, tapped out one last breakbeat on the table top, and rose to leave, I stopped him. I don't think I even knew what I intended to say until I heard the words coming out of my mouth.

His initial response was a mild grin that hovered somewhere between appreciative and condescending.

"Thanks for the offer," he said. "But it really wouldn't be appropriate."

"Why not?" I said, and stood up with him. For some reason, it surprised me to find that we were approximately the same height. "It'd be perfect. You'd be in a more convenient position, first of all. You've got angles from a floor and a half's worth of facing windows. And you wouldn't be exposed at all."

"Thanks," Doppler said. "But no. Sorry again for bothering you. Take care, now."

I ended up following him out onto the sunny sidewalk, unable to stop myself, feeling like an idiot.

"Listen," I said. "Help me feel better about this. I'm offering you all the comforts of your regular stakeout, plus a bathroom and a refrigerator."

"You don't even know what this is about," he told me. "You don't have any idea."

I shrugged suggestively. "So maybe you can let me in on a couple of the general plot points." When he didn't say anything, I added, "Or not, whatever. I'm just saying maybe I can help you out."

We stood there on the sidewalk watching the traffic go by. Doppler shoved his hands into the pockets of his faded khakis — the cuffs of which, I noticed, hung a good inch above the tops of his scuffed brown shoes. Here, I began to suspect, was a guy who counted on every paycheck.

After a long thoughtful silence, Doppler gazed back toward the restaurant.

"It's a terrible idea," he said. "But not actually the worst I've ever heard. I can give you twenty-five bucks a day out of my expense fees."

"That isn't even necessary. Seriously."

He nodded vaguely and looked at me in the bright noon sunlight. "It'll come out of expenses," he said.

"You're going to do *what*?"

"Sweetie . . . "

I reached out to take Erin's hand, but she pulled it back and planted it on her hip. Erin Slater semaphore for *you aren't even close to being off the hook.*

"Okay," said Doppler, from the doorway to my office. "Yeah. I should go."

"No, Jack — Jack." I motioned with my hand. "Just hang tight. It's no problem."

"Oh, no?" said Erin.

I nodded toward the kitchen and headed that way. When I looked back, Erin was still standing in the middle of the empty box-strewn hardwood we'd designated the dining room floor. Her arms were now folded. I tried a beseeching expression. She relented, following me into more private territory.

In a quiet voice, I said, "Come on. Don't you think you're overreacting just a little?"

Erin pegged me with her dark smoky eyes. "Well, let's see. Without a word to me, you've invited a complete stranger into our house, so that the two of you can invade the privacy of another complete stranger, who lives next door. Yeah, I guess you're right. I can be such a crazy bitch sometimes."

"He's a private investigator, Erin. He's got an ad in the yellow pages! I looked it up." It was true. I'd checked earlier, while Doppler was using the bathroom. His print ad was even less ostentatious than the business card, nestled almost invisibly in amongst impressive two-color banners for bonded commercial firms.

"Hooray for him." Erin's hand went back to hip again. She glanced once over her shoulder and dropped her voice. "I don't suppose it ever occurred to you that I might not be okay with this?"

"Erin . . . "

"Or did you just forget that I happen to live here, too?"

I decided the smart thing would be to say nothing.

Erin shook her head slowly, regarding me the way a fifth grade teacher regards a career problem student.

When I began to speak, she showed me her palm.

"Don't even say it," she said. "I know. I know."

"What?"

"I know you think this whole Mickey Spillane trip is just super cool, okay? But whoever this guy is, whatever's going on next door, it's none of our business. Plain and simple. It's none of our business, and you darned well know it."

"You mean you're not even the slightest bit curious?"

"We shouldn't be getting *involved*, Scott. I swear, I can't even believe you, sometimes."

We stood quietly for a moment. Erin had been doing her abs tapes three days a week; as a reward to herself, she was wearing a tight shortie tee shirt that showed a couple inches of flat midriff. I reached out a gave her navel ring a little flick. It was a sucker move. She'd always found it insanely ticklish.

Erin barked out a reflexive giggle, then bit it off at the root. "Goddammit," she said, slapping my hand away. "You quit it."

"It's only for a couple of days," I offered. "Tops."

"You haven't even been listening to me, have you?"

"Come on, babe. How many times does something this bizarre come along?" I tested out a little grin. "Besides. You're the one who's always saying we need to try meeting new people."

"Not through a zoom lens, freako."

"You're just as curious as I am. Admit it."

Erin merely continued shaking her head.

I nudged her.

Finally she sighed.

"I'm going to the movies with Amy. You and your new buddy . . . oh, whatever." She held up a single finger. "But let me restate, for the record: wifey does not approve. Seriously."

When I returned to my office, Doppler was sitting in the Stickley rocker and flipping through the new issue of *Advertising Age* magazine I'd gotten in the morning mail.

"Sorry about that," I told him. "Unexpected peace talks."

"So I gathered."

"Don't worry, Jack. I talked to her. She's cool."

"Mm hmm." He turned the last page, gave it a disinterested scan, and tossed the magazine back onto my reading table. "You spend a good portion of life doing damage control, don't you?"

That one caught me off guard. "What makes you say that?"

"Call it a professional conjecture," Jack Doppler replied.

BEING A GOOD WATCHER IS A BIG PART OF WHAT MAKES ME A GOOD COMMERCIAL artist. A half-smoked pack of cigarettes has a certain vibe. There's a slight, mysterious difference between a cell phone with a dead battery and one that's just about to ring. Sometimes there's a startling lack of visible difference between uncontrollable laughter and terrible weeping. Lust, envy, satisfaction, and uncertainty are in the spaces, not in the lines.

Think whatever you want about what makes it art and what makes it advertising. People buy what moves them. Only and always. I don't care if it's an emotion or a fib or a can of soda, it only leaves the shelf if somebody connects in some way. If a color isn't just right to the eye, it's just wrong.

That's where I find the art in what I do for a living. In the process of showing people everything they already know about the world. Sometimes, showing people what they want to *believe* about the world, in a way that seems so natural and familiar it somehow rings true.

I doubt I could think of a more illustrative case in point than Mumbo Gumbo, a local band the free weeklies say will almost surely be signing a record deal any second now. I know a little something about this band's history, and it's one of my favorite stories to pull out if a party gets dull. Assuming everybody in the room doesn't already know me. Which means I almost never get to tell this particular story anymore.

A couple of years ago, just as a way of testing out some new software I'd picked up, I designed a set of CD jewel case inserts for a non-existent band called Mumbo Gumbo. It was a goof, never intended as anything more — but the result turned out so incredible that it seemed like a crime to let it all go to waste. I mean everybody knows some act they think deserves a CD. But this was one CD that deserved an act.

Since I was a teenager, I'd always had this private fantasy of singing in a band. I'd never actually entertained the notion seriously — but all of a sudden, seeing that mocked-up disc case laying around my work space, the idea just started to burrow until I had to scratch the itch. So I got together with a couple of extremely talented musician friends of mine, who brought along a couple of their own extremely talented musician friends. And I pitched them all my idea, using this CD I'd designed for visual aid, and that was that. Mumbo Gumbo was born.

As soon as we had a set, we started getting booked all over town. I actually met Erin at one of our early shows, while she was still a nursing student.

After six months or so, the other guys voted me out of the band and hired somebody who could actually sing, but it was no big scandal. I said I was one of the world's great watchers. I never said I was one of the world's great lead vocalists.

We've all stayed great friends, I do all their graphic work for free, and Mumbo Gumbo has the coolest gig posters in town. Secretly, I kind of get a kick out of being the fifth Beatle.

As for that first CD? Cut and pressed. And it actually *has* gotten them a recording deal; the weeklies just don't know about it yet.

I don't kid myself. It's their music, and it really is unbelievably good. But we all know how the band got started in the first place. Maybe all of those guys would have gravitated toward one another eventually anyway. Who can say?

The point is simply that I've known for years being a good watcher made me a better artist. But it wasn't until I met Jack Doppler that I realized being an artist equipped me to be a better watcher.

Early on the morning after we'd met, he showed up at our front door just after Erin had left for the hospital. The first thing I did was take him back into my office to show him what I'd done.

Doppler — armed with his own coffee thermos, an uncased 35mm camera with a telephoto lens hung by a shoulder strap, and an overall presentation that suggested he'd slept in his clothes from yesterday — was visibly impressed.

"You've got to be kidding me," he said.

"So? What do you think? High tech, or what?"

I have an expensive color video camera that I occasionally use to run raw pre-production video into my main computer, which I keep upgraded with the fastest hardware available. Two beers and about an hour's worth of creative mounting and cabling, in the thin hours while Erin was asleep, was all it took to get the job done.

Jack stood with his thermos, gazing at the big 27" high-res monitor and shaking his head respectfully. On screen: a crisp, full-color image of my neighbor's house, angled on the facing corner for a partial view of the front door.

"What do I think?" Doppler finally said. "I think you strike me as a guy with way too much time on his hands. And that maybe I should hire you to come work for me."

"Here, check it out. If you want, you can train in tighter on any of these windows here on this side." I reached forward and showed him how to servo the camera and control the zoom and focus using keys on the computer keyboard. "You want any breakfast? I was just about ready to make some eggs."

"Thanks," Doppler said, eyes still glued to the monitor. He raised a pack of filtered Camels in one hand and hoisted his thermos with the other. "But I've got my breakfast right here."

"Suit yourself," I said casually.

But Erin was right. I really was just loving this to death. I guess I'd always assumed a real-life private investigator would be relatively uninteresting, at least by comparison to what you'd expect. More like, I don't know, your average claims adjuster than the rumpled rogues you got on television. But Jack Doppler was a walking wisecrack in a bad sport coat. As far as I was concerned, my office was his office for as long as need be.

I went off to find us an ashtray, wondering how hard Erin was going to hit the ceiling when she got home and saw we'd been smoking inside the house all day.

I SUPPOSE IT'S FAIR TO SAY THAT I DID ESSENTIALLY GO TO WORK FOR JACK DOPPLER over the next couple of days. And my office basically did become his office, at least for the time. He was extremely conscientious; he picked up his own empty take-out containers, he didn't smoke when Erin was around, and he took care around my gear. But it was his show all the way; I just hovered there.

I couldn't help but hang around. And while Jack never commented one way or another, I sensed that he honestly didn't mind the company. After the first day, he started asking me if I'd mind "watching the scopes," as he put it, for periodic stints. And I'd saddle up while he hit the bathroom or let himself sleep in the rocker a half hour or so.

The actual work of a private investigator, I discovered, was horrifically boring. But over the long hours — a vast dreary void of waiting and watching, hoping for a crummy blind to open or a curtain to rustle or *any* movement at all out of the guy next door — Jack gradually revealed enough to keep me parked in a chair right alongside him, punctuating the mind-numbing stretches of non-activity with jolts of coffee and nicotine.

"What do you know about a gal named Sharla Lake?" This was how he first opened the case for discussion.

What I knew about Sharla Lake was basically no more or less than anybody else who read the newspapers or watched local news. I knew that she was a scholarship middle blocker for the university's top five women's volleyball team. I knew she was a former teen beauty queen. I knew she was the daughter of one of the wealthiest families in the city. And I knew she'd been missing for almost two weeks.

According to Jack Doppler, Sharla Lake also was a young woman with a history of clinical depression; a troubled achiever prone to over-exercise and bulimia, whose struggle with her eating disorder had yielded a string of hospitalizations over the past several years; and a closet alcoholic who had, according to friends, boosted herself through her All-Conference junior volleyball season on a steady diet of crystal methamphetamine.

Her off-season strength training coach told reporters and police that Sharla had been missing workout sessions with increasing frequency. What the papers weren't saying, Jack told me, was that Sharla hadn't attended any of her classes on campus the entire week before the Lake family reported her missing.

And what neither the papers nor the cops even knew — yet — was that several days before Sharla disappeared, her younger sister had discovered the girl had been shooting heroin for almost four months.

"I got it from the Lake girl's best friend that she'd been seeing Raimer since before the holidays," Doppler told me, speaking of my neighbor, whom I'd never once seen since we'd moved in. "Guy's in his late thirties. Separated from a wife but not divorced, paying child support from another previous relationship. The two of them were keeping this little romance of theirs extremely quiet. My guess is, Warren and Marjorie Lake would not have been overwhelmed with glee."

"And you think . . ."

"I know she was getting her junk from Raimer. Word is he used to deal half the smack in midtown before he got hooked on his own merchandise. My understanding is that he mostly operates from the consumer end, these days."

"So do you think she overdosed? Something like that?"

"I did," Doppler said. "But the best friend got a call a few days ago. The call was blocked so she couldn't *69 it. But I've got a buddy at the phone company who owed me a favor. It looks like Sharla's been holed up at Raimer's place. At least that's where the call originated."

I couldn't believe it. Sharla Lake had been all over the news for days. And she was strung out next door? I peppered Jack with questions until he was fed up with answering them. Did the Lakes know their kid was okay? Why was he just sitting here, watching the house? Hadn't anybody told the police?

"Surely a bright guy like you can imagine the sensitivity," he told me. "Given the family name involved."

"Well, sure. Of course. But . . ."

"But, what? That's why a guy like Warren Lake hires a guy like me."

"But if you know she's over there . . ."

"Look," Doppler said. "All I know is what the best friend told me, okay? You want another professional secret? One of the first things you learn in this business is that only an idiot stakes a case on second-hand info. The friend could be the one screwing Raimer for all I know. Or maybe the guy left her for Lake. Or maybe he just sold her some bad shit and she's seeing a chance to scrape him up a bit."

"But I thought you said . . ."

"Hey. Do I think any of that is what's really going on here? No. Do I think Sharla Lake and Larry Raimer are probably passed out over there in the dark with needles hanging out of their arms? Sure I do. And the first glimpse of wavy blonde hair I see, that's what I'll go tell Warren Lake."

Once I'd repeated the story, even Erin got interested. On day two, Saturday night, she actually canceled on her romantically struggling friend Amy to stay in, drink beer, and watch the neighbor's house with Jack and me. Erin and I drank the beer. Jack Doppler stuck to coffee, explaining with one wonderfully short, mysterious sentence that he didn't drink anymore.

After several hours — enough time for Erin to get an honest taste of the stakeout experience — she came right out and asked him what I'd been dying to ask since I'd learned what Doppler was doing in this part of town.

"Why don't you just go over there, knock on the door, and drag the girl home already?"

"Because that's not my job," Jack Doppler said. "I was hired to find a girl. On Monday morning, I'll tell the girl's parents everything I know. They'll pay me. And I'll go home. It's up to Warren and Marjorie Lake to decided what to do from there."

I said, "I still can't believe that guy's a junkie. He's got the best looking lawn on the whole block."

"Yeah, well," said Jack Doppler, taking Erin's permission to light a cigarette. "You're the ad man. You of all people ought to know the way things look ain't always the way they are."

DOPPLER'S STAKEOUT ENDED EARLY SUNDAY EVENING. HE WAS IN THE OFFICE, reading a JD Salinger biography of mine while he sat in front of the monitor, feet propped on an unpacked box of books. I was in the kitchen putting on another pot of coffee. And Erin was upstairs in the bedroom, folding laundry and watching television.

And all at once, she started shouting.

I came out of the kitchen and called up from the bottom of the stairs. "What's so exciting?"

"The TV!" she shouted back. "Turn on the television. The news! Channel 5, hurry up!"

I hustled into the office, dug around in the mess for the remote control, then gave up and went over to the rollaround cart to turn on my little color set by hand. Erin was already tromping down the stairs.

Jack glanced up from his book. "What's up?"

"Dunno." Stooped at the waist, I punched all the way down from channel 30.

By the time I got to the news, Erin had joined us. The screen was filled with a color studio headshot. The photograph portrayed a gorgeous young girl with soft blonde hair and smart hazel eyes and an easy, heartbreaking smile. It was the same photo of Sharla Lake the papers had been running. Just as we tuned in, the photo receded to a thumbnail in the upper right corner by the anchor guy's head.

We only caught the end of the segment, but I heard enough to get the main idea. Sharla Lake wasn't missing anymore. At first, I'd assumed they'd found her dead. But apparently, she'd returned home to her parents house herself early Sunday afternoon.

Somehow. Right under our noses.

"They said she's been in California," Erin said, breathless and disbelieving.

"Staying with a friend. I guess she freaked out about something and just took off without telling anybody."

"Freaked out?" I couldn't believe it. "What do you mean, freaked out?"

"They didn't say."

Erin and I turned to look at Jack Doppler at the same time.

He was still staring at the television. His eyes seemed oddly blank. He didn't say a word.

I said, "Jack?"

And at the sound of my voice, while we stood there watching, Jack Doppler's face seemed to fall in on itself. I'm not sure how else to describe it. His expression simply . . . sank, like a collapsing meringue.

"Jack," I said.

Erin took a step toward him. "Jack? Are you all right?"

Without a word to either of us, Jack rose from the chair. He looked at the television for a moment longer. Then he collected his thermos and cigarettes, shouldered his camera, and slouched out of the room.

Erin and I traded glances and followed. He was already letting himself out the front door.

"Jack!" I called, from the steps. "Hey, Jack. You okay?"

But Doppler just kept shambling on, shoulders stooped, arms hanging loose at his sides. His thermos dangled from one hooked finger like a mitten from a child's cuff.

"What's he doing?" Erin said.

I was at a loss. "Search me."

What he did stunned us both to silence.

While Erin and I stood and watched, Jack Doppler crossed our driveway, climbed the gentle rise on the opposite side, and trudged through Larry Raimer's front yard. He mounted the steps to the front door.

Paused there a moment.

And let himself in with a key.

I looked at Erin. She stood beside me, head dipped forward, her mouth hanging open wide.

We watched him pull the door shut behind him, cradling his thermos close in his other arm. A half second later, the sound reached us, a muffled thud that disappeared as if swallowed by the air.

WE MUST HAVE STOOD THERE WATCHING FOR AN HOUR OR MORE. JACK DOPPLER never re-emerged. Erin and I eventually wound up in my office, pressed together in front of the computer screen, hashing and rehashing this bizarre turn from every angle imaginable. The whole thing was just such a mind twist that I don't think either of us could decide how to begin processing it.

We stayed up trying for hours.

Every so often, my recurring impulse — to charge over there and bang on the door until somebody came out and explained themselves — flared to nearly intolerable levels. Erin stood behind her own instincts and argued against the idea tooth and nail. But I knew the impulse was hollow anyway, our debate a frustrated grope for resolution. Defense mechanism of the soundly rooked? Maybe so. But deep down, I knew I wasn't going anywhere.

I kept watching the monitor until long after Erin had fallen asleep. Whenever I saw a light come on behind a curtain, I picked that window and zoomed in. I panned and scanned and sat there like a paranoid night watchman with a Heineken buzz.

And eventually, at some unknown point, I finally conked out, too. I don't think I realized I'd fallen asleep until I woke up with my head on my arms and a wide puddle of drool on the desk beneath my face. It was six AM, just dawn. Erin's alarm wouldn't sound for another half hour.

Maybe some part of my REM-locked consciousness had sensed activity. Or maybe I just heard the sounds through my office window, which I'd propped open with the Salinger biography the night before.

Whatever woke me, I lifted my head just in time to see, on screen, Jack Doppler leaving the Raimer house through the side door.

Bleary and cotton-mouthed but coursing with indignation, I was outside to meet him by the time he reached the sidewalk. He was on his way to the crappy white Ford Tempo once again parked on the opposite curb.

"Hey," I called. "Hey. You hang on a second."

Doppler paused to look at me. The first thing I noticed was his eyes. Gone was the unusual clarity I'd noticed in the gyro shop three long days ago; his pale blue gaze now seemed . . . clouded. Strangely diffuse. This morning, Jack's was the vague unfocused gaze of a person who is either far past the point of exhaustion or deeply, deeply stoned.

Gone also was the ill-fitting sport jacket. In its place: a faded gray work uniform. A round patch over his right breast pocket said RAIMER AMOCO. A dark blue jot of embroidery over his left pocket said GLENN.

After a moment, his dull eyes flickered and brought forth a distant grin.

"Oh, hey," he said. "How's it going?"

"How's it *going*?" All I could do was stare at him. "What the hell is this?"

Jack — Glenn — just looked at me like he didn't understand. Then he shrugged and shuffled past. "Okay. See ya."

I heard the sound of a door opening, the jangle of a fat ring of keys. I looked up and saw another guy emerging from the house. He pulled the door shut behind him and descended the concrete steps.

I stalked across the dew-soaked lawn and met him in the middle of his own flagstone path. He had damp reddish hair parted at the side and a close-trimmed beard carpeting his jaw. Late thirties. Shorter than me. He wore a dressier Polo-style version of the same Amoco shirt. Above the left pocket: LARRY. Beneath the name: OWNER.

"Can I help you?"

"What is this?" I demanded. "Is this supposed to be some kind of joke?"

He leaned back and put up a hand. "Easy, pal. I don't know what you're talking about."

I jerked my thumb over my shoulder. "I don't know what you guys are trying to pull, *pal*, but I don't appreciate it. I should call the police."

It wasn't until after I said it that I remembered Officer Ray from the gyro shop. I was beginning to loose my cool.

But Larry Raimer just kept his palm raised and looked at me like he had no idea what he was supposed to say. We stood there facing each other — me in dew-soaked socks and hair on end, him assaulted six feet outside his front door by a stranger with fermented morning breath.

And then he had it. I could see the recognition in his eyes.

"You must be the new folks next door," he said.

"Scott Brady," I muttered. I yanked my thumb back once again. "And *he* is?"

"That's my brother," Larry Raimer said. "Glenn." His tone was heavy with something. Something that sounded to me like well-practiced apology. He sighed. "I take it he's already introduced himself."

"Oh, you could say that," I told him. "Only the guy I met called himself Jack Doppler."

"Discreet Private Investigations," Larry Raimer recited, as if to the sky. "I know. I know."

At this point, I was past words. I just stood there looking confused. When Raimer offered his hand, I shook it mechanically.

"Listen, it's nice to meet you, Scott. And I apologize for . . . well, for whatever. I really do. Sometimes I take it for granted that most everybody around here already knows Glenn."

I could feel myself unclenching, my blood cooling from boil to simmer. Seeing the look of tired sincerity on Larry Raimer's face, I took my pot off the burner altogether.

"My brother has . . . challenges," Larry Raimer offered, before I could think of something to say. "I guess you've probably figured that out by now. Did he cause any damage? If he did, I'll certainly cover it."

"Damage?" I felt myself shaking my head no.

Larry Raimer seemed genuinely relieved, if not exactly surprised. He talked for a bit, explaining for me what he'd so obviously explained many times before.

While he never actually got into the clinical specifics of his brother's condition, I got the sense that clinical was the only adjective that applied. Over the years, Jack — *Glenn* — had spent time in a variety of private facilities. He did well at none of them, and Larry had gradually lost his ability to stomach the sight of his brother inside those walls. He'd been looking after Glenn himself for the past three years.

"He's mostly okay when he takes his medication," Raimer explained. "But I'll tell you, it's heavy-duty, the stuff they've got him on. We're talking serious scouring power."

I nodded.

"Shit just stomps the juice right out of the poor guy. Sometimes he stops taking it." Raimer apologized again with his eyes. "I used to really lock him down, but I've learned it works out much better for everybody if I just let him get it out of his system every now and then. Buddy of mine runs the Super 8 out on Industrial Road. He makes sure Jack Doppler has a room whenever he comes in."

I looked at Larry Raimer. For some reason, I chose not to tell him that Jack Doppler had been using our couch for a motel room since Friday.

Raimer looked back at me and sighed again. "He's basically harmless. I know that probably doesn't mean much to you."

This I waved away. Since I'd calmed, I'd begun to feel just a bit like what I'd been five minutes ago: an asshole on the rampage. "You run that station up the street by the sandwich place?"

Raimer nodded. "Ten years now. Glenn works for me in the garage. He really is a pretty good guy to have under the lift, when he's not playing Magnum PI."

I looked over toward the curb, where Glenn Raimer waited patiently in the passenger seat of the rusty white Ford.

I knew I shouldn't ask, but I couldn't help it. "Does he . . . I mean, does he really . . . ?"

"Does he really believe he's Jack?"

I nodded. Feeling, for some reason I couldn't quite identify, like an intrusive shithead for asking.

But for a moment Larry Raimer seemed to consider the question himself. For perhaps the hundredth time. He finally looked up and said, "Some days, to tell you the truth, I honestly can't tell. I mean the guy can be pretty doggone creative when he wants to be."

"I'll say."

Raimer smiled. "But deep down? Way down deep I think there's a part of him that always knows it's all a game."

We stood together for a quiet moment, watching Jack Doppler's troubled imagination waiting in the car, his eyes turned toward the closed passenger window, watching two squirrels fight over something in the grass nearby.

I said, "What do you think the gets when he wins?"

"I'll bet I've asked myself that question a thousand times," Larry Raimer replied. "I don't know the answer, but I'll tell you something. I think the only time my brother is ever really happy is when he feels like he and Jack are uncovering something."

I didn't know what to say to that. So I didn't say anything. After another beat, Raimer looked at his watch.

"I really need to get up there and open the shop," he said. "Nice meeting you, Scott. And I really am sorry for any trouble. You want to come over for a cold one some night, maybe you can fill me in on Jack's latest case."

I told him that sounded like a plan. He nodded and headed for the car. As he stepped off the near curb, he looked back over his shoulder and said, "By the way — welcome to the neighborhood."

It took us a month, but Erin and I finally got ourselves situated in the new house. Though our studio apartment had been packed to the rafters, in the new place we barely had enough stuff to completely furnish one entire floor. But we each had a room of our own that felt like your own space should feel, with plenty of room to grow together, plenty of echoing spaces to fill.

I found myself buried under three new contracts. Erin's friend Amy talked her into signing up together for pottery classes at one of the community colleges two nights a week. We stayed busy.

I didn't make it over to Larry Raimer's. I did take the video camera down. Raimer and I would nod and chat for a minute whenever we happened to be out in the yard at the same time. I didn't see much of Glenn.

But those first weeks following the Sharla Lake case, I found myself thinking about him at the oddest times. I thought about how hopelessly intriguing I'd found Jack Doppler. About how convincing a character he really was.

I marveled that I hadn't seen so much as the faintest seam in Glenn Raimer's costume persona. I wondered if there would ever come a time when he'd no longer be able to find the zipper himself, once he'd put it on.

But mostly I thought about what Larry Raimer had said that morning in the sidewalk while Glenn waited in the car. *I think the only time my brother is ever really happy is when he feels like he and Jack are uncovering something.* I wondered what that must feel like, and it poked at my heart imagining.

Erin always tells me I get bored with my own life too easily, but I don't think that's true. The truth is, I love my life. I just happen find the rest of the world irresistibly fascinating.

And for some reason, I found I couldn't stop wondering what it must be like for a fellow like Glenn. To live, forever and always, in a world for which you were fundamentally unequipped. A world where nothing offered even a measure of the joy or solace you found in the world you made up as you went along.

I don't know if what comes next actually answers the question or just asks it another way. I don't think I really know anything.

All I know is that it was a Wednesday night. Erin and Amy were at their pottery class. As for me . . . I was sitting in my office, as Jack Doppler might say.

And when I went to answer the doorbell, there he was. Standing in a pool of yellow from the overhead light, decked in his out-of-style sport coat and flood-water khaki pants, reaching out to press the doorbell again.

"Mr Brady," he said, when I opened the door. "Sorry to just drop in. I was planning to call first, but I was in the neighborhood."

I couldn't help but smile at that. "Hey there, Jack. Long time no see."

"Mind if I come in?"

I thought, *oh, why the hell not?* I held open the door and he came inside, noticing as he passed that he carried two manila envelopes.

I asked if he wanted coffee, but he only thanked me and shook his head no.

"It took a bit longer than I'd expected," he said. "But I think I've got what you were looking for."

"Oh, yeah?"

He held out one of the envelopes. I was too curious not to play along. I put on a serious face, took the envelop, moved to the couch and sat down to unwind the strings. After I'd removed the contents, I decided the game was over. Maybe Larry Raimer was right. Maybe Glenn was basically harmless. But enough was enough.

"Okay, Jack. This is getting out of hand."

I was looking at a series of black and white photographs, developed in a home darkroom into six-by-nine prints. The photos were of Erin, and they looked like they'd been taken at a variety of locations. Three outside a restaurant I didn't know. One in the parking lot of the AMC movieplex on the West side of town. Two appeared to have been snapped from behind a bush in a park somewhere.

In all six, Erin was with Paul, a friend of ours. Paul is Mumbo Gumbo's bass player; he and Erin had been pals since before Erin and I even met, and I knew they still caught a movie or a bite to eat every now and then.

"Really," I said. "This isn't cool, okay? Do you understand?"

Jack Doppler nodded along as though he understood completely. But he still handed me the other envelope.

"I'm sorry," he said.

I opened it because I needed to see just how far he'd gone with this newest delusion, how severely he'd violated Erin's privacy.

And that's when the bottom dropped out of the world. A cold, creeping numbness started somewhere in my groin and spread from there.

"I know this probably won't make you feel any better," I heard Jack say, somewhere in the buzzing distance. "But for whatever it's worth, it hits just about everybody the same way. I've seen it . . . well, too many times."

I stared at the pair of photos in my hands. Only two, in this pack. One wide-angle. One tight shot that must have been taken with at least a 400 millimeter zoom.

In the wide angle, even though it was night, I recognized the dent in the rear quarter panel of my friend Paul's car.

In the tight shot, I couldn't be absolutely certain. But I was pretty sure Erin was wearing her lacy black shirt.

She wasn't exactly wearing it. The perspective of the shot was looking in through the back window. I couldn't see Paul's face, because he was somewhere behind her.

I wished I couldn't see the expression on Erin's. But considering the distance and the lighting, it was an excellent photograph.

"It doesn't matter what you suspected," I heard Jack say. "Or what you already knew. It's still a kick in the lunchbucket."

I don't think I even knew I was swinging until I felt something pop deep in my fist. By the time I realized I'd completely lost it, my hand was already bouncing off Glenn Raimer's concrete skull. The photographs slid across the slick bare living room floor.

Jack Doppler barely even flinched with the impact of my pathetic flailing. In the charged breathless moment after I hit him, some part of me thought he might reach over and break my skull. But I didn't care. I just stood there, beginning to shake, sick with rage and adrenaline.

But Jack maintained his professionalism. He didn't retaliate. In fact, he didn't even so much as frown. His face remained passive, his eyes calm and clear. He reached up and touched the tiny spot on his cheekbone where my knuckle had split the skin. It wasn't even bleeding.

Before he turned to go, Jack Doppler looked at me with what I could only interpret as condolence. Or maybe it was pity.

After he left, I sank back into the couch and stayed there for a long time. I looked at photographs. At some point, I got up to get some ice for my swelling hand. I came back and looked at photographs some more.

Erin's friend Amy must have skipped pottery class, because she answered the phone when I called. I hung up without saying anything.

Mostly I just sat in the dark, alone in our new house, approaching midnight on a Wednesday, watching the front door.

I decided I was going to watch until it opened.

I'm one of the world's great watchers.

THE HOUSE OF DEATH
PAUL DOHERTY

A magnificent new murder-mystery series featuring Alexander the Great

It is 334 BC and the young Alexander waits with his troops by the Hellespont, poised to attack the empire of the great Persian king, Darius III. To win the approval of the gods for his enterprise he makes many offerings, yet the smoke does not rise, the sacrifices are tainted. Worse, his guides are being brutally murdered, Persian spies are in the camp, and Alexander's generals have their own secrets.

Into this turmoil comes Telamon, a physician, and boyhood friend of Alexander. As the climax builds and Alexander throws off his nervous fears, winning a brilliant and bloody triumph over the Persians, Telamon at last succeeds in uncovering their enemies.

Paul Doherty is the internationally renowned author of many historical novels. He studied history at Liverpool and Oxford universities, and gained a doctorate at Oxford. He is now headmaster of a London school, and lives near Epping Forest.

- **First in a new series of historical mysteries featuring Alexander the Great**
- **Paul Doherty has published many hugely successful historical novels and murder mysteries**
- **Follows the enormous success of the historical mysteries of Steven Saylor and Elizabeth Peters**

Superb reviews of Doherty's previous books include:

'The Mask of Ra is the best of its kind since the death of Ellis Peters. As ever, Doherty dazzles us with his knowledge and intimate feel for ancient Egypt.'
Time Out

'A rare example of historical fiction that isn't overloaded with history and doesn't give supense short shrift.'
Publishers Weekly

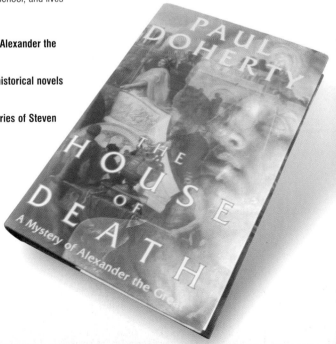

House of Death
Paul Doherty
28 June 2001 hardback £16.99
1 84119 302 X Constable

CONSTABLE

milo and i

antony mann

Antony Mann has had three stories in previous editions of Crimewave, including 'Taking Care Of Frank', which won the 1999 CWA Short Story Dagger. He is currently working on a screen treatment for 'Shopping' (CW4). It looks like being a pretty short film.

"Listen Milo," I said. "You stink."

Milo chose to say nothing. I was talking to hear my own voice speak, that was all. Bottle in hand, he fixed me with those big dopey brown eyes of his and cackled like a loon. Then, for a second I thought he *was* going to reply, but when he opened his mouth, it was only to stick the bottle back in. He took a long, deep suck and burped appreciatively. He was near enough bald as an egg, always had been.

"What's the matter?" I said. "Cat got your tongue?"

"Cat!" he said, looking round the room expectantly.

"No, no cats here, Milo," I said. No cats. There was the body of a man, though, lying spreadeagled on the cream-coloured living room carpet, a neat bullet hole in the middle of his neat forehead. At the back of his head it wasn't so neat. Forensics were still tweezing shards of his skull out of the pile. The man could have been fifty. It was hard to tell with him laying there, his right leg splayed out at an odd angle to the rest of him, but his build looked small to average. His silver-grey hair was short and styled in layers. That day he'd chosen to wear black shoes, grey slacks and a black collarless pullover. Apart from his white skin and the dried blood, he was black and grey all over. Even in death I could tell he'd been a smoothie.

Sergeant Woodstock saw me now and sauntered over. Except for the uniform, he might have been a builder with a fondness for the wrong kinds of food. "This is a crime scene, Detective McCann," he said. "What's with the baby?"

"Cat!" said Milo, wriggling in my arms, trying to escape. He was only thirteen months old, he wouldn't have gotten far.

"No, no cats here, Milo," I repeated. "We'll go see a cat later. If you're good."

"The kid stinks," said Woodstock.

"Just what I told him. He needs his nappy changed. Want to do it?"

"Thanks but no thanks," said Woodstock. "Had enough of that over the years at home watching the wife. Milo. What sort of a name is that for a kid?"

"Same as for an adult, only younger," I said.

"Couldn't find a babysitter?"

"We're on the job," I told him. "It's the new pilot scheme."

"Oh yeah. I heard about that. I thought it was some kind of a joke."

"If it is, I'm still waiting for the punchline."

The thing of it is, a good detective always looks at a case through the eyes of an innocent, without baggage or prejudice, giving equal weight to all the facts and the evidence. But how many good detectives are there any more? Three? Five? Nobody knows for sure, but the consensus is, less than ten. And I'm certainly not one of them. That's where Milo comes in — and for the rest of the detectives who need them, the other babies in Project Wide-Eyed. Milo is supposed to be my lost sense of wonder, my permanently impaired fascination with the mundane that went out the window as soon as I got my driving license and applied for my first credit card. Don't get me wrong, some things still fascinate me. At last count, three: women, sport, and booze. The last makes the first more fascinating still, and the second is what I watch to fill in time between the first and the last. When I get lucky I can combine all three.

"So who's dead?" I asked. Now that he knew Milo was on the case, Sergeant Woodstock talked to the both of us. In a way, being my partner, Milo outranked him.

"Max Cassidy. Fifty-two years old. Owned a small chain of furniture stores in the south-east. He was married, but estranged from his wife the last twelve months. No kids. Lived here on his own. Looks like the killer knew him. No sign of forced entry or a struggle. Whoever was holding the gun fired it from close range." Woodstock looked at Milo. "Want me to repeat anything?"

"Cat!" said Milo.

"We'll take a look around," I said.

Woodstock was aghast. "You can't just let a baby crawl around where there's a guy been shot! Even if he is on the team!"

"Who said anything about crawling? He can walk holding onto furniture."

"You don't have kids of your own, right?"

"Not that anyone's told me about."

"Listen to someone who's got four. Kids see enough violence on TV without exposing them to it in real life. Come back in an hour, okay? Go get yourself a sandwich. Or some rusks." On this one, Woodstock outranked *me*.

"I'll go change his nappy," I said.

MAX CASSIDY'S NORTH OXFORD HOUSE WAS BIG, AND THE LIVING ROOM WAS BIG too, twice as long as it was wide, with a high ceiling. It was marginally less cluttered now that Cassidy's body had been removed. The crime scene team and Sergeant Woodstock had also departed, leaving just Milo and me, some bloodstains, and too much furniture. It looked as though Cassidy liked to bring his work home and sit on it. There were some antiques, but there was junky stuff too, a lot of it, and in no particular place or order. Broad glass doors at the back afforded a view of a neglected sweep of lawn that led the eye on towards a small and unhappy apple orchard at the bottom of the garden. High brick walls protected the neighbours from the unsightly mess. There was money here, but not much regard for what it could buy.

"For such a neat dresser, Cassidy sure was a pig," I said out loud.

"Pig!" exclaimed Milo, looking round the room expectantly.

"No, no pigs here, Milo," I said. "Maybe we'll go see a pig later. If you're good. Now, look for clues."

I put him down on the floor, took a seat in the luxurious olive green leather armchair near the bigger of the two bookcases, and watched him go. He went. He was in a kind of baby heaven, allowed to do all the things that he would never have gotten away with at home. He pushed things over, then fell over the things he'd pushed. Other stuff he turned upside down. There was a pile of old magazines in a cardboard box in the corner. He emptied them out, got in the box, then emptied *himself* out. He stood in front of the smaller bookcase across the room, and one by one pulled the books from the bottom two shelves. At one point he opened a faded hardback by some forgotten writer and sat there staring at the words on the page, pretending to read like he'd probably seen his parents do. Then he looked at me and laughed, like he'd just cracked a joke. After which, he tried to stick the book in his mouth. All of it.

Frankly, watching him, I was envious. He had no words for most of the objects he was pawing at and bumping into, no emotional baggage, just a powerful drive to experience and learn. To him, everything was miraculous and new. I tried to put myself in his shoes. What was he seeing and feeling? He was pulling papers off Cassidy's bureau, and I watched as he examined each one minutely, as though it must contain some remarkable and transforming secret, but I got only a glimpse. That door was all but shut to me now. In Max Cassidy's house Milo and I were exposed to same stimuli, but to make any real impact on me, they had to sneak past all my defences, my ingrained ways of thinking. My jaded, desultory world-view. Now that I thought about it, my life these days was a process of keeping things out. That didn't seem good. Suddenly, I felt depressed.

"Ah ah!" said Milo, interrupting my thoughts. He'd found something. He was crawling over to me with a sheet of paper in his gob. I took it off him.

"What is it, Milo? What you got?"

"Baby!" he said, smiling gleefully up at me.

It was the newsletter of a charity, ChildAid. The name rang vague bells. A few key phrases leapt off the page at me: '. . . letting them have the life they deserve . . .', '. . . protecting the innocent . . .', that sort of thing. I flicked over the page. Inside, among other things, was a black and white photo of Max Cassidy, illustrating a short article. As a prominent and community-minded local businessman, Cassidy had recently accepted a non-paying directorship on ChildAid's board.

"Well, well," I murmured. "Cassidy joins charity, and a few weeks later gets popped by jealous fellow fund-raiser. What do you think, Milo?"

"Baby!" he said. I turned back to the front of the newsletter. In the top left hand corner I saw what had caught Milo's attention. It was ChildAid's logo, a stylized image of a baby girl, smiling dreamily as she peeped out a gap in her swaddling clothes. Milo had simply been attracted by a picture of one of his own kind.

I gave him the newsletter to play with while we drove to the supermarket. He was running low on formula.

SHEILA CASSIDY LIVED ACROSS TOWN IN EAST OXFORD, IN ONE OF THE SOLID OLD 1930s terraces in Hurst Street between the Iffley and Cowley Roads. She opened the door to my knocking. Max Cassidy's widow was a slim and elegant forty-five, with angular features and the soft, well-maintained hands of a non-worker. Her short hair was wavy and dark, interwoven with a few unconcealed strands of grey that suited her. Her breasts were just about on Milo's eye level as I held him, and I caught him sizing them up through her creaseless white blouse. He looked disappointed. She wasn't the welcoming type, but after I'd explained who we were, she managed to invite us in off the front step. I could tell she was having a stab at politeness when she asked if we'd care for a drink.

"That's not necessary," I said, "but I'll have a white coffee, no sugar. Milo likes one part orange juice to three parts water in a non-spill cup, if it's no trouble."

"Milo," she said, regarding him with indifference. Her voice was educated and clipped, "What sort of name for a baby is that?"

"It's the sort that makes people ask what sort it is," I said. Her smile was mirthless as she led us through into the living room and went to get the drinks. Sheila Cassidy's tastes were modern, and spartan. It wasn't a huge space, but she had made the most of it by whitewashing the walls and decking them with abstract prints, the kind with the artist's name at the bottom so you know it's not just a scrawl by some no-talent nobody or a trained monkey. There was no carpet, only bare boards stripped smooth and stained and lacquered to a nice matte finish, although a thin woven rug lay on the floor between the dark green sofa and matching easy chair.

There were books on white modular shelves — a few modern novels, but mainly coffee table dross by the looks — and a rack of classical CDs near the sound system.

Telling Sheila Cassidy that her husband was dead went a lot better than I'd hoped. The news, in fact, appeared to make her day, and after the initial jolt of surprise, she even warmed a little. "Dead, you say?" she said, chirpily. "Violent, was it?" She sat in the easy chair while Milo and I hogged the comfy green sofa.

"Shot in the head with a small caliber handgun," I told her. "We're extremely sorry to be the bearers of the news. And I'm afraid that we are going to have to ask you some questions at some point. If you'd prefer, we could come back tomorrow when you've had a chance to . . ."

"No, no, may as well get it over with," she said briskly. "Any suspects other than myself? I was at bridge club all morning, if that helps to eliminate me. And there have been no large cash withdrawals from my bank account of late, so I doubt it was me who hired any professional hitperson, if such a person did it. Not that I'd know about such things. Of course you'll want to check my alibi, so I'll give you my bank details and a contact number for the club." While she paused for breath I took out my notepad and began to scribble. Milo tried to grab the pen off me, perhaps to make observations of his own on the wall or furniture. Sheila Cassidy went on, "We've been married sixteen years, separated for the last one. Why? Perhaps we simply drifted apart like so many couples nowadays. Or could it have been the succession of bimbettes he screwed senseless both in and out of our home in a series of cruel affairs, for which in time I could have forgiven him had he made any attempt whatsoever to hide them from me in consideration of my feelings? Who can say which it was? No children, we never wanted any. So. Max is dead."

She looked round the walls of her living room, as though they were perhaps a little too close together, characterised by a narrowness which might soon be remedied by a move to a far bigger house — of a size to which she had once been accustomed — thanks to a sudden influx of funds from Max's own supply, as of that morning no use to him at all.

"Do you mind if my partner takes a look around?" I asked her.

"Will he break anything?"

"No more than any other police officer," I said. "Maybe less. He can't reach the high stuff." To be fair, there was precious little in Sheila Cassidy's living room for Milo to wreck. He crawled around for a bit, searching for leads, then tried to climb her leg. I give her credit for not shaking him off. "These . . . bimbettes . . . with whom your husband associated," I said. "Can you remember any of their names?"

She flung her arms into the air. "There were so many! And you know, it's not the sort of information that I made a point of retaining. But there was one. Belinda Costello. I remember her because she came to the house once to confront me when Max was at work. She announced that they loved each other, and that he was going to leave me for her, and there was nothing I could do about it." She laughed. "As if Max ever loved anybody. Stupid cow!"

"Cow!" said Milo, letting go his grip on Sheila Cassidy's ankle long enough to look around the room expectantly.

"No, no cows here, Milo," I said. "We'll go see a cow later. If you're good. Mrs Cassidy, I don't suppose you know where your husband met this Belinda Costello? How we might get in touch with her?"

AFTER I'D DROPPED MILO OFF AT HIS PARENTS FOR THE NIGHT, I WENT HOME, blasted a packet of frozen meaty gloop in the microwave, grabbed a bottle of beer, and settled into my favourite chair in front of my favourite television. Tonight was Champions League night on terrestrial, so I turned down the lights, let the tension seep out of my brain, and waited for the small flickering screen to cast its spell. Five minutes into the game, I realised I was still restlessly thinking. It was the case, nagging away at me. No, not the case — it felt like Milo and I had made good progress — it was Milo himself.

There was a picture in my mind which wouldn't go away: I could see Milo, sitting on Max Cassidy's floor with a piece of dried, shrunken orange peel in his hands. On his face was a look of utter amazement, as though he had just happened upon a jewel of incomparable value and beauty. Such innocent wonderment. Such *joie de vivre*. He was truly alive. Me, I had a beer in my hand, Arsenal were on the box, and I was dead. Luckily, not dead enough to ignore the sudden pang in my heart. Was it an ache of loss? Regret? Indigestion? On impulse, I reached for my mobile and punched in the number that lately I had been getting to know pretty well. After a few rings, Kristen picked up. "Look, not tonight," she said when she realised it was me. "Mum's over. How about tomorrow?"

"I didn't want you to come over," I said. "I just wanted to talk. Even for a few minutes."

"Talk?" She sounded confused. "Talk about what?"

"I don't know. Things. Like, isn't life amazing?"

There was a pause. "Who is this really? Is this a crank call? Because I'm warning you, my boyfriend's a police detective."

"No, Kristen, it's me. I wanted to talk about life, that's all, about how incredible it can be, how everything you see, everything you touch, can be the most amazing experience you've ever had. If you can only open your eyes and . . ."

"Are you on something?" she asked suspiciously.

"As a matter of fact, I am," I said. "I'm on my chair. Now that I look, there's a little ketchup stain on the arm that I hadn't noticed before. It's shaped kind of like a butterfly, and it's tacky to the touch. Next to it, about an inch away, is a small tear where something sharp has jagged into the material. And beside that the loose thread is poking up where one of the buttons has come off . . ."

"Call me back when you're sober," said Kristen.

The line went dead. But there was still a ketchup stain on the arm of the chair.

BELINDA COSTELLO HAD WORKED FOR MAX CASSIDY AS A SALESPERSON IN HIS Oxford furniture showroom for nine months back in 1998. Sheila Cassidy had told us as much, and Ms Costello herself confirmed it as we sat in the cosy living room of her house in the village of Bladon, six miles north of Oxford itself. It was where Winston Churchill had been buried, alongside the rest of his dynasty under slabs in the small churchyard on the slope of the hill. Frankly he couldn't have asked for a prettier place. The dwellings were out of an age before housing estates and building-by-numbers, with uneven frontages of council-protected stone that faced onto twisty, narrow laneways. The village was picture-postcard, yet un-affectedly so. Residents might have been conscious of the history they had bought or been born into, but they had no desire to sell it, and so there was no sense of the terminal quaintness which afflicts the commercially ravaged heritage hotspots.

We had found Belinda Costello at home that morning with what she had claimed was a bad cold, though to me, as she perched on the edge of the armchair part of a cream and olive two-piece, it looked more like a nasty hangover. Whatever the truth, if anything the pallor of her face and the circles under her eyes enhanced her striking Italianate beauty. She must have been about thirty. Her skin was smooth, her hair was dark and long and rippled around her shoulders. She had made no apologies for her slippers and tracksuit, and why should she? She would have made anything look sexy, even complete nudity. I could see why Max Cassidy had been interested. I could see why anybody would be, although Milo was probably a little young.

"So you left Max Cassidy's employ in November of 1998 and took a job in real estate." I was sitting on the divan. "Why was that exactly?"

"I wanted to move up in the world. Instead of selling furniture, I wanted to sell the big things that you put furniture in." She was smiling at her little joke, yet not looking at me at all. The whole time, her eyes were fixed on Milo as he crawled round the room, poking and sniffing at things. Now she looked at me, "Actually, it was because of Max. You know about the affair, right? That's why you're here?"

"That's right."

"When it ended, I thought it was the best thing to move on."

"And who was it who ended it, Ms Costello?"

"He did."

"Why was that?"

"You'd have to ask him. Oh, sorry. You can't. He's dead." She gave an odd little laugh, then turned her attention back to my partner. "He really is a cutie. Milo. What a lovely name."

"Yeah, that's what everyone says. I just hope it doesn't go to his head. When was the last time you saw Max Cassidy, Ms Costello?"

"The last time? I guess that would have been a couple of months ago. I was shopping one day in Oxford and I bumped into him in the — "

"Ball!" Ferreting in the narrow space under the divan, Milo had come up with something. It was a screwed up ball of paper that he emerged with.

"Oh, sorry about that! Now how did that get there?" Belinda Costello was off her chair in an instant, but I had spotted something on the paper, and grabbed it out of Milo's hands before she had a chance to.

"It's okay, I've got it," I said, unfolding it and smoothing it out on my leg.

"Baby!" said Milo.

"So it is, Milo, so it is."

I was holding another copy of the ChildAid newsletter — there was the baby girl logo on the top left hand corner. I opened it to the middle two pages. Someone had taken a sharp implement, most likely a knife, and stabbed the photo of Max Cassidy fifteen or twenty times. His face had been completely obliterated.

"Well, how would *you* feel?" Hands on hips, Belinda Costello stood over me, her soft and beautiful face contorted with sudden rage. "Max Cassidy told me he loved me, which was just fine until he got me pregnant! He all but forced me into an abortion, then as soon as I'd gotten over it, he dumped me! And then, this!" She ripped the newsletter from my hands, screwed it up again, and tossed it across the room.

Milo crawled after the evidence. "Ball!" he said.

Belinda Costello was getting wild. "Letting them have a decent life? *Protecting them?* After what he made me do? What was that, some kind of sick joke? I killed my own child for him! He was nothing more than a dog!"

"Dog!" said Milo, looking round the room expectantly.

"No, no dogs here, Milo," I said. "We'll go see a dog later. If you're good."

I stood up. Belinda Costello's fury was spent, and her shouts were turning to sobs. I looked at Milo, playing happily on the carpet with his paper ball. He would have been about the same age as her own child, maybe a little younger, if it had survived. I wanted to put an arm around her, comfort her, tell her that I understood, even a little, how she had felt and why she had done what she had done. As an alternative, I arrested her.

"I HEAR THAT MILO ALREADY SOLVED THE CASSIDY CASE." SERGEANT WOODSTOCK set his tray down opposite mine, took a chair, and proceeded to obscure his fish and chips under a layer of ketchup. I'd seen it before, but not usually at breakfast. I drank some coffee. Woodstock was still talking: "That's a real fillip for Project Wide-Eyed. Word is they're going to bring it in all over the country. And they're converting one of the broom cupboards here into a baby change room."

"The kid got lucky," I said. "Sometimes that's what it's all about. Luck. A lucky break. A stroke of luck. Dumb luck. Beginner's luck. He lucked out. Say it how you like."

"Not what I heard," said Woodstock.

"Why? What's he been telling you?"

"Not a lot."

"No." The canteen was humming with pre-morning shift conversations. "Still, the way the kid works, I reckon I can learn a lot. I reckon we all can. Finding that newsletter screwed up under the divan was no accident. He saw it and went for it. No hesitation at all. 'Ball!' he said, and grabbed it."

"It wasn't a ball, it was a newsletter," said Woodstock.

"Close enough. Apparently since he joined this ChildAid mob Cassidy had been sending these leaflets out to everyone he knew, soliciting donations. Costello got hers, and flipped because of the abortion thing. Went round to see him the next morning on a pretext and shot him in the head. Brutal."

"Yeah, but when you think about it, maybe Cassidy got what he deserved. Sounds like he was a real snake."

"Snake!" I said, looking round the room expectantly.

I SAT WITH MILO AT THE SQUAD ROOM WINDOW, HOLDING HIM STEADY AS HE PERCHED on the inside sill, his tiny hands flat against the pane, looking out onto the station carpark. "What is it, Milo?" I whispered in his ear. "What do you see?"

"Bird!" he said.

And there it was, a common starling, brown as mud, swooping in from the west, doing nothing really, just swooping and flying, being a bird, as it lighted an instant on top of the compound's chainlink fence, before taking off again to disappear beyond the further edge of the cell block wall, out of sight. Together, we watched it go.

"I see it, Milo," I said, "I see it."

And, maybe just a little, I did.

six miles from earth

brady allen

Brady Allen lives and writes in the
inspiring four-season weather of Ohio,
and shares a home with his wife, two-
year-old daughter and giant, insane
attack cat. He teaches fiction writing
and general literature (Great Books) at
a state university in Ohio. He's part of
a quartet of writers (The Mudrock
Writers) who have been meeting
every Monday for three years to help
each other out, and so he wants to say
hello to Jimmy Chesire, Rita Coleman
and Scott Geisel. Brady is currently
working on a novel called Take One at
a Rolling Donut, about Rose Holmes,
who appears in this story.

From my mother's sleep I fell into the State,
And I hunched in its belly till my wet fur froze.
Six miles from earth, loosed from its dream of life,
I woke to black flak and the nightmare fighters.
When I died they washed me out of the turret with a hose.

Randall Jarrell, *The Death of the Ball Turret Gunner*

THE CAR SLID ALONG THE FLAT TWO-LANE ROAD LIKE A GROUND-SKIMMING SILVER
bullet. Words danced in Rose's head, words about black flak and nightmare fighters
— a short poem from a community college poetry class she had sat through with
a hangover. Jarrell, that was the poet's name. It'd been months since then, months
that seemed like years.

She whispered the words over and over and watched the pavement rise and fall
through the cracked spider web of front windshield.

She tapped her fingernails restlessly on the steering wheel, wriggled her ass on
the warm fabric of the seat, chewed on her bottom lip.

Black flak.

She *refused* to cry.

The desert flats droned on and on, and she touched the rim of the bottle of
Irish Whiskey to her lips, letting the last of the liquor drip on her tongue. "Fucking
Amen," she said absently. "Thank you, Grimm."

She tossed the empty bottle onto the passenger side floorboard, and then reached
over and grabbed the pack of Winstons from the seat next to her.

Had to clean it out with a hose.

She punched the cigarette lighter and shook a nic-stick from the pack, tossing
the others back on the seat. "This is the most monotonous fucking place on earth,"
she grunted, glancing out the passenger side window, rolling the cigarette back
and forth between her thumb and forefinger as the desert spread out around her,
endless and mostly flat. "We'll do it around here, Grimmy. We'll do it around here."

The sun was directly in front of her, and the gray Buick's visor dangled listlessly
in front of her face. She pushed it back up into place and watched it slide back
down slow and sneaky-like. She was topless, wearing only a pair of faded jeans
and her long black boots. The blood red radiance scorched through the glass and
simmered on her fair skin. She could feel a slight tingling, a burn building in her
breasts. She peeked around the limp-dick visor and hugged the yellow centerline.

The lighter clicked and sprung back, and she slid the Winston between her shiny
crimson lips. She grazed the tip with the coils of the lighter and inhaled deeply,
holding it in and then letting it out in a burst, smoke hanging momentarily like
a storm cloud and then twisting away violently and disappearing out the open
side window. She pushed the lighter back into its hole and laid the cigarette in a
groove in the open ashtray.

A hose. Washed him out with a hose.

She turned on the Buick's radio, twisting and tuning the dial, searching. She
stopped the radio on some static that was accompanied by intermittent flashes
of electric guitar. She retrieved the cigarette and left it dangling from her lip like

a cancerous, fire-tipped white worm. Her foot rested heavily on the accelerator, the thick black boot keeping the speedometer dial right at 80.

The rearview mirror was angled down, revealing the back seat, but she never looked into it, though she heard the wind whipping the blankets and plastic that covered the cloth interior.

Black flak.

Fiery prisms of devil red and angel white sunrays bounced through the cracked windshield. She watched the yellow line through the pinpricks of schizophrenic light and saw a dead rabbit, its entrails smeared along the road. "Oh shit, honey-bunny," she said out loud and then giggled. "Sawmbawdy kilt a wabbit, Gwimm."

She splashed dryly through black watery mirages on the road, and a head of cigarette ashes dropped onto her pale breast. She flicked them away absently and started to look more closely for a promising exit. She needed a truck stop, a juke-box, a cup of thick black coffee. That was where she'd want them to find her. That was where she was comfortable.

But first, she needed a velvet Jesus.

Hunched in its belly. Its belly.

Rose leaned forward and crossed her arms over the top of the steering wheel. A pickup truck passed by on the left, heading the other direction. Driving in the daytime gave her a bitch of a headache. She had dry-chewed her last aspirin hours ago. She ground her teeth together and enjoyed the sensation of her breasts pressed against the hot, hard plastic of the steering wheel. She drove this way for ten or fifteen minutes, smoking cigarettes, squinting into the sunlight, watching the yellow line, glancing up when she came to a single side road, but passing it by because of its brightly colored, well-lighted service station.

Another ten minutes and she saw a sign, an old billboard, weathered and faint:

SIX MI TURN RIGHT   GAS EATS
ENTERTAINMENT TRAILER PARKING

She eased back against the seat, taking a long drag on her cigarette. That's where she'd stop — an exit too small to have a name. And they'd better have a gas station where she could steal a fucking velvet Jesus.

Six miles from earth, loosened from its dream of life. Six miles . . . Sick smiles!

(Wow, that was crystal clear — was that you, Grimm? Grimm?)

Things were looking up. She could sense salvation beyond this asphalt, beyond this sand wasteland. She flicked her ashes into the tiny ashtray under the radio, and she smiled, a real honest-to-sweet-Jesus smile. Things would be okay.

From my mother's sleep I fell . . .

The road to food and a velvet Jesus slanted off to the right and she could see it, the rest stop, if that's what it might call itself, squatting there in a little block of buildings. As she took the road in, she noticed that all of the buildings were plain except for one — a ranch style building with a painted sign on its roof. The sign had a woman with a tiny skirt that was flipped up in back. She was backing into an obviously phallic cactus and had a big smile on her face. There was one word on the sign, in big red letters: PRICKY'S.

There were six buildings total — Pricky's, a gas station to its right that just said FUEL on its block wall, two unidentified residences a little bit behind everything (maybe a hundred yards or so), and a gray building to the left of Pricky's that said only XXX ADULT. And, lo-and-behold: an honest-to-God greasy spoon of a diner.

Rose swung the Buick up along the pumps at the gas station, shut off the engine and reached down to the floorboard for her shirt. It was a plain white T-shirt, and she slipped it over her head and pulled her thin arms through the short sleeves. Her nipples rubbed lightly against the cotton fabric as she stepped out from the car and reached her arms back behind her, stretching, fingers laced and locked together.

She relaxed and stood there for a moment, trying to look in the front window of the white block building. But there was a glare on the glass, and she couldn't see inside. She didn't pull the license plate down yet, so she could unscrew the gas cap hiding under its grimy HUR 696.

First she needed a velvet Jesus.

Don't . . . don't fall into the State.

Rose walked toward the entrance of the building marked Fuel. The thick glass front door had a black sign with white trim, and orange letters proclaimed the establishment to be open.

Outside the door she looked up into the expanse of sky. The sky is only something to fall from, she thought. Dreams hurtling through empty air until they eventually hit the ground somewhere in the world, only to be stepped on like hot chewing gum on asphalt. Our own dreams are annoyances to other people, and they get picked at and scraped a little before they are tossed away.

Will they wash my trunk out with a hose? My back seat?

Bells jingled on the door as Rose pulled it open and walked inside. A faint blanket of cool air swallowed her, and goose bumps broke out on her arms. Her nipples stiffened beneath the cotton of her T-shirt. She saw a blocky air-conditioner rattling and vibrating in a small window toward the rear of the room.

A man who looked to be about forty or fifty sat behind the counter and stared at her out from under a black NASCAR cap. He was playing solitaire on the counter space next to the cash register. He looked down when she met his eyes, and he flipped through cards and slapped them on the counter without saying a word.

Rose scanned the aisles of overpriced Pringles and M&Ms, Moon Pies and Wrigley's Spearmint, looked past the row of motor oil, antifreeze and other car maintenance products. A wire rack sat in a corner and held postcards and bumper stickers. Next to it on a wooden shelf were some framed pictures. She walked down an aisle and stopped in front of the shelf. Behind her she heard cards being shuffled. A cooler kicked in and shuddered, bottles singing out softly as they bumped into each other.

There were several prints of an old mining shack and one of a coyote with its snout turned to the sky. A photo of a bikini-clad girl straddling a motorcycle had smudgy fingerprints all over the glass in its frame. There was a stack of Denver Broncos football pennants, and turned sideways behind the stack was a velvet picture — not Jesus though.

Elvis. A velvet Elvis.

Rose thumbed through a few more frames — another woman humping a motorcycle, a picture of the cast members from *The A-Team*, several copies of a drawing of Monica Lewinsky smoking a stogie.

No Jesus. Not a single one. Just a velvet Elvis.

Loosed from its dream of life.

It'll have to do, she thought. She picked up the frame and turned it over, more out of habit than intention. $10.00, a sticker read on the back. "Elvis Christ," she pushed out through her teeth and then giggled. She had a pocket full of change and didn't think the shufflin' dude would be much for bartering anyhow. Besides, some things were just habit.

Rose unbuttoned her jeans and looked over at the guy playing cards. His head was tilted down and cards smacked the counter in the unspectacular rhythm of a bored man. She looked down at the picture. Elvis was frozen in a pelvic shake on the velvet canvas, his arms out to his sides, fingers extended.

Rose slipped the frame down the back of her Levi's and pulled her T-shirt down over it. She walked stiffly for the door, pushed it open without looking back, and made it about two steps out into the bright sunlight before a hand grabbed her arm roughly from behind.

Wet fur froze.

She tried to rip free, but the grip was strong. She turned and kicked out wildly, the frame poking and digging into her back. The man laughed as her foot glanced harmlessly off his leg. He jerked her toward him, spinning her around violently. She heard a click and then the blade of a knife was pressed against her throat.

"The King don't come free," the man said as he walked her back into the building.

Back inside the store, the man locked the door behind them. He reached down the back of Rose's jeans and pulled the velvet Elvis free. Rose watched him slap it onto the counter and recalled a sign she'd seen somewhere. A porno shop in Vegas maybe. ALL SHOPLIFTERS WILL BE EXECUTED.

"So what's it worth to you, gal?" The man kept the knife pressed against her neck.

"Fuck you." Rose was calm, surprisingly calm. But then again, nothing could compare to what the trunk of her car held, nothing could compare to the events leading up to that. Abso-fuckin-lutely nothing.

"Close, gal. And I'll give you a cigar anyhow." The man pushed her around behind the counter, and threw her to her knees on the smooth concrete floor.

He reached under the counter and pulled out a handgun. He pressed it to her temple and tossed the knife onto a table against the wall. "I think you know what you owe me, gal."

He pinched his zipper between his thumb and forefinger and pulled it down. Rose noticed that the denim was grimy and worn thin around his crotch. "C'mon, gal," he fairly whispered, pressing the gun more firmly against her head. Part of Rose said to do something stupid — anything. Anything to make him just put a bullet in her head. Just end it right here. But she was tougher than that, had a will to live, to fight.

From my mother's sleep . . .

Besides, she had something she had to do first. An obligation out there in her car.

The man slipped his fly open, undid the snap, pulled his jeans down to the tops of his thighs, his dingy briefs with them. His dick was already hard — short, thick, and veiny. He cupped his free hand behind her head, pulled her face forward, the gun still pointed at her skull.

Rose grimaced and complied.

He came quick and weak — little dribbling pearls on her tongue. And when she stood up, wiping her mouth, he laughed at her. "Take the fucking picture," he sneered. "You're paid up in full, gal." She snatched the picture from the counter and walked around and out the door.

And just a moment later, she walked back in and the man barely had time to look up from his cards as the bells jingled. A smattering of buckshot ripped through the NASCAR logo on his cap, bits of scalp, gray matter and splatters of blood spraying against the wall behind him. Pieces of bone fell to the floor like pebbles.

Rose reached across the counter and turned on the gas pump and then walked back out with her sawed-off still smoking.

The velvet Elvis sat in the back seat like an idol on a shrine. The plastic and blankets were now wadded up in the floor, and splashes of dark crimson decorated the gray cloth back seat. Rose walked around to the back of the Buick and flipped the license plate down. She leaned the sawed-off against the bumper, and then she pulled the nozzle from the pump and locked it into the groove in the plate. Gas flowed like white wine into the Buick's tank.

I hunched in its belly . . .

Rose slipped out of her white T-shirt and tore it into long, even strips. She finished ripping it just as the pump clicked off. She tied the ends of each strip together until she had one long, white length.

A couple of men had come outside and were standing on the porch of the building with the Pricky's sign. Maybe they had thought the loud sound was backfire from the car because they didn't budge. They only watched her, probably hoping she was going to come inside.

Rose opened the trunk.

There was Grimm, her boyfriend, her man, her love. Straight from the morgue — right under the nose of the goon with the Walkman who was manning the desk. She ran her fingers through his hair and leaned over to kiss him softly on the lips. They were bloated, swollen, purple. She caressed his skin; it felt like old damp parchment as she trailed her fingers along his chest.

Wet fur froze . . .

She could taste the events from not so long ago: the robbery gone bad. The old fuck having a gun. Grimm having taken a bullet in the gut, screaming in the back seat, bleeding like a stuck pig. And Rose, driving, hearing sirens close by, pulling up in front of the hospital, and rolling Grimm onto the sidewalk out front, kissing him quickly, and rolling away with a squeal of tires.

She kissed him harder, deeper, and remembered: the shit hole hotel room, the television . . . "Robbery," the man said . . . "One assailant died today in the hospital" . . .

Rose pulled her lips free from his and kissed him on the forehead. "It'll have to be Elvis," she said. She knelt down at the back of the car and pushed one end of the white strip of cloth down into the gas tank. She was shielded from the two men by the trunk lid. She ran the length of torn T-shirt along the side of the car and in through the driver's side window. She doused the entire strip with gasoline from the nozzle and then walked back and gave Grimm one last gentle kiss.

She walked around to the passenger side door. Rose was careful not to let the two men on the porch see her breasts. This was a moment for her and Grimm. An intimate moment. Religious. A moment that demanded respect. Let them stare all they wanted later.

She slid across the cloth interior, leaning over into the driver's seat, and wondered if it was cold in hell. She looked over her shoulder at the velvet Elvis. "Christ forgive me," she whispered.

Wash the fucking thing out with a hose . . .

The white T-shirt length hung down to the floorboard, and she picked it up and spread it across the seat until it rested on her thigh. "Lab animals," she whispered as she pushed the cigarette lighter in. And she had a brief vision of a morgue with cages.

She opened the door and stepped back out onto the asphalt, and then she leaned back in and pulled out the lighter. She looked at the glowing orange coils.

Six miles from earth . . .

She touched the lighter to the wet white cloth before she walked, naked from the waist up, toward the greasy spoon, hoping to at least get herself that cup of coffee and drop a couple of coins in the jukebox.

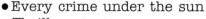

THE THIRD ALTERNATIVE

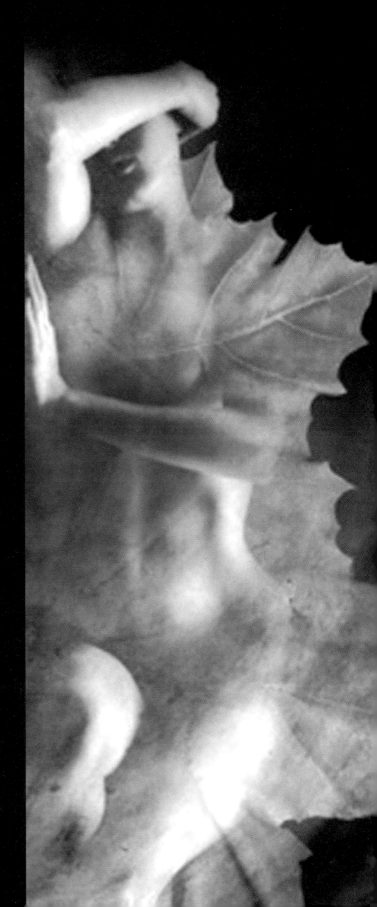

Quite simply, if you enjoy Crimewave you'll enjoy The Third Alternative. You get lots of stunning original artwork by the likes of Mike Bohatch (right), Joachim Luetke, Rob Middleton, Roddy Williams, David Ho, Menglef, Chris Nurse; interviews with novelists such as Geoff Ryman, Jonathan Carroll, Joyce Carol Oates, Peter Straub, Luke Rhinehart, Clive Barker; a film column by Christopher Fowler; comprehensive review coverage of the latest books; and plenty of extraordinary new stories by writers such as Muriel Gray, M John Harrison, Simon Ings, Michael Marshall Smith, Mark Morris, Christopher Priest, James Lovegrove, Graham Joyce . . .

'The most exciting new work is being honed on the cutting edge between genre and mainstream. TTA stories are definitely the best of contemporary short fiction'
Time Out

'Vibrant, lyrical, beautiful'
The Guardian

The Third Alternative is beautifully designed and presented — A4, 68 pages with colour laminated cover — and a six-issue subscription costs only £18 (£21 Europe, £24 RoW, $28 USA), payable to 'TTA Press' and sent to the Crimewave UK or USA editorial address. Single issues are £3.75 (£4.25 Europe, £4.75 RoW, $7 USA)

Funded by
THE ARTS COUNCIL OF ENGLAND

eastengland|arts

face value

shelley costa

Shelley Costa's fiction has appeared in The Georgia Review, Crimewave 4, The North American Review and Cleveland Magazine. She holds a PhD in English and has most recently taught creative writing at the Cleveland Institute of Art and major American writers at Case Western Reserve University. Along with her husband and the youngest of their three daughters, she lives in Chagrin Falls, Ohio, and gets away for a month in the summer to the Canadian Northwoods, the setting of her new novel. 'Face Value', the first in the Carmine Angelotta series of mysteries, is in memory of her father, who grew up on Macdougal Street in Greenwich Village at a time when gin was no farther away than your bathtub.

WHAT THEY TEACH YOU ABOUT SEX AT ST RITA'S WHERE MY BROTHER PAOLO AND I went to school is, of course, nothing useful in the classroom and nothing factual on the playground, which meant we were left trying to make sense of fallopian tubes and how French kissing can lead to pregnancy. This information we discussed on fire escapes with our pals Mookie Mendez and Yitzy Schreiber and Donny G. It became clear to us, finally, that there was no substitute for on-the-job training, a position shared by Bunny Burgoyne to the everlasting gratitude of the five of us boys known throughout Greenwich Village as the Macdougal Street Strays.

But even Bunny, and the ones who followed in the fifteen years since, had nothing to say on the subject of what it is about womanhood that dries the mouth and whittles the male heart like a soft chunk of wood. Bunny was far from my mind the night I was minding Paolo's flower shop while he paid his new wife a conjugal visit over in their apartment on West 12th. Paolo, it turns out, came up with two mutually exclusive ideas: getting married and keeping the shop open until midnight to catch what he hoped was a fleet of late-night customers — the wayward, the sheepish, the achingly romantic. So most nights, for want of anything better to do, I tape up a note saying where to find me and then I mind Paolo's store, which is not a hardship, considering I live and work upstairs behind the frosted glass door that says Angelotta Investigations.

I was still cleaning up broken glass and spilled water from a drunk who had come in at eleven-ten, staggered backwards around the shop, having mistaken it for a bar, swung his walking stick into a floor display of bearded irises, and left. I'd pay Paolo myself for the damage. The shop was too stacked with breakables to get into it with a drunk. Cleaning up helped pass the time until midnight when I could close. I propped open the swinging front door to let in the night air and the traffic of Macdougal Street, where an early June night made it possible for tired lovers and the chronically lonesome to stroll. There were horns and shouts, scrills of laughter, music released from nearby bars as doors opened and closed.

I was crouched near the door, carefully laying the biggest shards of glass in my hand, when she came in. She was narrow and golden and silent. Nothing I learned fifteen years ago literally at the hands of Bunny Burgoyne prepared me for this sudden certainty that sex, like God and major league baseball, is beyond our understanding. No sooner did she take me in than she crossed her arms and sidestepped me with a smile that lasted just the right amount of time. "Evening," I heard myself say as I strung together what appeared through a light sweater to be the beautiful boniness of her shoulders and a soft blue skirt that lay next to every inch of legs so long they disappeared into kingdom come. Some clothes have all the luck.

She circled the cheap bouquets and backed away from the carnations. I swept up the rest of the glass and stuck the irises in with a dried flower arrangement. We arrived at the cooler at the same time. She cleared her throat, which I took as a sign I made her nervous. The crossed arms, the cleared throat, something about a thirty-year-old dark-haired guy in jeans, high tops, and a pretty clean T-shirt in a cramped flower shop was getting to her, but it was nothing I was going to question. She said, "Can I see the lavender roses?"

I opened the cooler slowly, trying to figure out how I could parlay handing her a rose into as much skin contact as possible. I pulled out the three best and turned back to her. Her eyes were on me in an appraising way. I twirled the stems gently, then handed them to her, just brushing her chin. She didn't flinch. It was a statement. Only I didn't know the language.

"For yourself?" It was my turn to cross my arms.

"No," she said, looking them over.

I felt my eyes narrow. "A friend, then?"

"No," she said, handing them back to me. The buds were loosening, their petals rounding open at the base like they were filling invisibly with water. "I don't think you have what I'm looking for."

Were we still talking flowers? I waited a few seconds for the real subject, then, disappointed, returned the roses to the cooler. "How do you know?" She lowered her head, thinking about it. "You only just got here." Her hair fell to either side of her neck, and I felt a spasm of love for her, but she took a step away from me, pushing a tortoise shell comb deeper into the thick tangle of her hair. Her eyes took in the entire shop. Suddenly I was ashamed of Paolo for not having a proper flower market with carts of dahlias and Peruvian daffodils. The most beautiful woman I had seen on Macdougal Street in the last ten years was about to slip out through the swinging doors. I leaped to the desk, pushing around the FTD books. "Would you like to be added to our mailing list?"

She stopped. "You have a mailing list?"

"New. A new one. We tell you about specials." I grabbed a gift enclosure card and pushed it toward her with a pencil nub. "There you go," I said as she started to write. When she finished, I turned the card to me: Catherine Coleman, One Sheridan Square.

She had a name.

She had a place to live, just a few blocks away.

She had nice penmanship.

She lay down the pencil and smiled for only the second time, then headed for the door. "I'm looking for something different."

Different from lavender roses?

NEARLY TWENTY YEARS AGO WE STRAYS USED TO SWING FROM ROPES TIED TO THE fire escapes outside the third floor windows of the Mendez and Schreiber apartments. Yitzy's family lived just around the corner, so his home made a nice right angle to where the Angelottas and the Mendezes lived. We called the uncut grass and cracked concrete and discarded appliances 'the courtyard'. Eventually the washer and the electric range got carted away, but every summer someone planted petunias in the toilet, so it stayed. Mr Mendez, a mad longshoreman, brought the ropes home from the docks the summer we were eleven, and rigged them to the railings with good bowline knots, smoking and muttering in Spanish about 'el peligro', while helping us to a fair taste of el peligro all the same. For the next four years, Mookie, Yitzy, Donny G, Paolo and I swung out over the courtyard with the reckless joy of boys who needed nothing less than the possibility of sudden god awful death to take their minds off the mysteries of the female body. Tess Angelotta, our second cousin from the next block of Macdougal Street, was the only girl. We let her come because she bore the Angelotta name, which made her the women's auxiliary of the Strays.

When it came to the ropes, we begged her not to, we dared her to, ignored her when she tried to, and clamored for her praise when we took our turns. "Carmine," she told me in a fierce, quiet way that was my first glimmer that girls had passions the rest of us knew nothing about, "I can do it, you know." When she finally got her turn the second season, the rest of us feigned boredom while she tied back her long brown hair, so we didn't really notice when she slipped her foot through what we called the tricks loop that gave us a toehold for airborne spreadeagles we made look harder than they really were. Tess jumped, having pushed the loop all the way up to her knee and I nearly wet my pants when she turned herself upside down as the arc took her high over the courtyard. The others goggled. "Lookit her leg!" Donny G pointed. "Tess!" I screamed, seeing her leg loosening in the loop. "Tess!" I climbed down to the next landing to try to reach her, to pull her in, but not before I saw on her face the awful victory she felt.

I hated her a little for making me see a place inside where terror lived — but I hated the rest of us more for whatever it was about being male that made her feel she had to risk her life to win our attention. "Tess, Tess," I grabbed her, furious, as she swung close to the second floor fire escape. We clawed at each other while Mookie leaned out like a dancer, gripped by Paolo, to free her leg from the rope. Then, because I couldn't hold her I shook her, and because she couldn't hold me she bit me in two places and we wrestled on the fire escape, throwing soft punches that we embellished with a lot of grunting, until Paolo pulled us apart and she and I sat there, shaking, against the railings until nightfall.

On the ropes, we all had our styles. Yitzy flailed, trying complicated maneuvers that never worked. Donny G would try latching his knees over the railings for whatever private reasons, probably fear. Paolo was elegant. I was dashing, doing lame spreadeagles in every possible direction. But Mookie was the best. Mookie was the only one of us with the strength and nerve to do what we called the old Tarzan switcheroo, sailing over on one rope and grabbing the other, which one of us, standing on the Schreibers' fire escape, would fling out over the abyss toward him as he came. It was a feat of great daring and precision, and it was Mookie's alone. His family were Basques who had come from Spain two generations ago, and in his mind he associated the ropes with the mountain life in his family history, although nobody knew why. We couldn't touch Mookie on the switcheroo. We honored his Basqueness.

When the elder Mendezes died a few years ago, and his kid sister Serafina just a year ago, Mookie kept the apartment and turned the bodega they owned on the street level into Mookie's version of a curiosity shop. He bought out discontinued items and closeouts wherever he could find them and resold them in Mookie's Novelties. Cheap nylon flags from countries that no longer existed, naked lady ashtrays and letter openers, phallic candles, roach clips and rolling papers, Japanese brass balls I was still trying to figure out, lava lamps, beaded curtains, studded collars with and without chains, and religious bric-a-brac, everything for the wiccan consumer. Out-of-towners came in and gawked. Locals kept Mookie in business.

The store was dirty, considering what some of the stuff was intended for, although Mookie himself showered ruthlessly. Every day, regardless of the weather, he wore black jeans, leather vests, silver-studded cowboy boots, and one garnet earring that had belonged to Serafina. His black hair was shaved close to his head, but what was left over his forehead was gelled permanently vertical. On his chest hung a silver crucifix the size of Excalibur. He belonged to no political party, attended no Masses, read Garcia Marquez in the original, and was celibate. So, apparently, was I.

"Mookie," I told him the day after Catherine Coleman turned away from my lavender roses, "I'm in love."

A local user with a concave chest lurked at the back of the shop, where Mookie kept the cheapest novelties too far from the front counter for him to know or care whether they went out of the store in pockets instead of shopping bags. Still, we kept our eyes on the guy. "So, Carm," he said. "Who is she?"

WE ATE FELAFELS TOGETHER IN THE STORE, MOOKIE AND I, AT SIX, WHEN THE STREET business died for a while, then kneaded each other's shoulder in a way that said ain't life hell, ain't life grand, ain't nobody a better friend than you. Outside I tossed the crumpled wrapper in a trash basket, and went up the street to Angelotta Investigations. Mine was a red door with peeling paint that opened on sagging wooden steps. I thought it had charm, but as Polly Angelotta Stanhope, my mother, figured it: how would potential clients think I could find cheating spouses and runaway kids if I couldn't even find a can of paint? She forgot that over the past five months I had found a cat, a mistress, a birth mother, and a runaway. The cat paid the best. I was halfway up the steps when I was surprised to hear the street door open. Muffling a burp with my fist, I turned, figuring it was Tess or Mookie.

Catherine Coleman stared up at me, her face tight. I leaned against the wall as she started up. "You're Carmine Angelotta?"

"Yeah. You finally figured out what you want," I said as she drew up next to me, "and it's still not lavender roses."

"It's help. I need your help."

So yesterday she was just checking me out. "You want to come up?"

"I'm being blackmailed."

Not what you want to hear from your intended, since blackmail, in my experience, is some smart cookie's way of capitalizing on the truth. With Catherine Coleman's looks, fifteen years ago it would have been snapshots — show-all poses for more than pin money to a high school girl who now realized she had some Anglo Wall Street dad to protect. Or an affair with a high-profile married man. If those were the circles of Catherine Coleman, I would charge top dollar because I could kiss goodbye the fantasy of a house in Scarsdale and two new little Angelottas. I give family discounts, even future family discounts, but I am all retail mark-up when it comes to women sleeping with other women's husbands. It was how my mother became a Stanhope and moved off Macdougal Street to East 59th. I had no use for it then and no use for it now. By the time I had let us both into my office apartment, I chilled toward my intended and practically flung a chair at her.

She sat.

I leaned in front of her against my desk, taking in the hands laid out on her lap, the nails trim and unpolished. She huffed a couple of times as she lowered her head and I waited, then strolled behind her, wanting to rush her over to my futon and make all the trouble disappear. If Catherine Coleman was being blackmailed it was because she had made what she thought was an anonymous donation of historic proportions to UNICEF and some kid-hating accountant had sniffed her out.

"Two years ago I had an affair — " there went UNICEF " — with someone at work."

"So?"

"It was . . . inappropriate."

"You mean wrong?" If there's one word I hate, it's 'inappropriate'.

She looked straight ahead at something far away, past Umberto's across the street, past even the China Sea, wherever the hell it was. "Are you a moralist, Mr Angelotta?"

Just moral, I wanted to tell her, but it sounded prissy and I wasn't sure it was always true, so I said no, but I knew that wasn't exactly true, either. So I moved on. "Letters? Calls? What are you getting?"

"Letters. They started three months ago."

"How many?"

"Six."

"And — ?"

She shivered once, then looked me in the eye. "I've paid eighteen thousand dollars."

Stunned, I slowly pulled myself up on to the desk. "Do you have that kind of money?"

She nearly smiled. "Not any more."

"Where do you send it?"

"A different address each time. But it's always one of those private mailbox companies."

"Do you have the letters?"

"I threw out the first two, thinking I was done." Her hand flopped in her lap.

"You're never done."

Catherine Coleman licked her lips. "So I see." She straightened up. "After the fourth letter, when I sent the money, I went to the address the day I expected it to show up and hung around outside. Nothing. Or, at least, nobody I recognized. I went inside finally and asked if Mr Milton — "

"That's his name?"

"Different names every time."

"Go on."

"Asked if Mr Milton had picked up his mail. They told me Mr Milton had left a forwarding order and no longer got mail there. So my payment — " she looked at me " — got forwarded to an address they were not at liberty to say."

"What did Mr Milton look like?"

"They had never seen him. He did everything in writing, opening the account, forwarding his mail, everything."

She looked like she could use a drink, only I had never offered one to a client. I could help her *pro bono*, which might do our relationship some good, but not my checking account, so I decided the best thing altogether was to offer Catherine Coleman a beer and charge her my most uptown fee. She accepted all my terms, I handed her a Sam Adams, and she walked to the long, low windows that overlooked Macdougal Street. The soft skirt whispered around her hips as she moved.

"So, Ms Coleman, what do you want me to do?"

She sipped, her eyes still on the street. "I want you to tell me the name of the blackmailer."

"And then?"

"There's no 'and then'. All I want is the name."

"No confrontation? No counter threats? No police?"

"No. Your job ends with the name."

I couldn't figure it. "Then what makes you think you'll ever be done paying?"

She took a long swallow, and I liked her for it. I liked the way she held the bottle and eyed the contents. She looked straight at me. "What makes you think I ever expect to?"

ONE-TWELVE AM, THE WINDOWS OPEN, THE CEILING FANS CIRCULATING THE AIR SO thick it felt like breathing through wet cement where I lay alone on my futon. In the alley across the way, garbage cans clattered. Sirens went by, the night birds of New York City. I couldn't sleep without them. But then — I kicked off my sheet — I couldn't sleep with them, either. From where I lay I could see past the rooftops on the east side of Macdougal clear to the crescent moon. The letters Catherine Coleman left me were strewn over the bed, the closest any part of her had gotten to my sheets.

It was blackmail with no new features, as original as a Barry Manilow song lyric. *I know, pay up, don't tell.* On white printer paper sold by the case in any office megastore. A default font on a common word processing program on a PC you could buy at a discount store. Nothing distinctive about the stamp, the envelope, or the typed address. The postmarks were different zips, but always Manhattan. All she added to the letters was the fact that, up until last year, when she had joined the staff of Bank Street Psychotherapy Association, she had been a school psychologist at Waverly Academy, a local boarding high school for the sons of the Manhattan aristocracy. A man — here she paused — named Hugo Kilcannon was headmaster. Under no circumstances was I to approach Hugo. He was off limits. His wife, Maude, was a thoroughly sweet woman with ovarian cancer who needlepointed coverings for the school library chairs.

"Kilcannon," I said, taking useless notes. "Age?"

"Forty-seven." No hesitation.

"Children?"

"One. A son. Dexter."

"How old?"

"Seventeen? Eighteen?" she said. "He'd be a senior at the school."

I hardly listened while she said a few words about the list of students and co-workers she handed to me. "Why did you leave?"

"I needed to end it."

"And if you hadn't?"

Her eyes went to the floor. "It would have become public."

"You're being blackmailed, Ms Coleman." I set down my empty bottle. "It did."

"Not in the same way."

"If the blackmailer found out, so did others — but only one of them wants to turn a profit."

She was silent long enough for the light to shift as the sun went down. Shadows appeared, faint, as I watched Catherine Coleman master whatever she felt about the affair with Hugo Kilcannon and the last two years of her life. "All I want," she said finally, "is the name."

"Why?"

She stood. "Because, Mr Angelotta, quite a lot of my money has been taken by somebody I trusted. I'd like to know who."

Six hours later, well after midnight, I switched off the goose neck lamp by my bed and walked in the dark to my open window, where I stood stiff-armed with my hands on the frames, leaning into the night air. It was a legion of sorrows down below on Macdougal Street. There was Yitzy Schreiber, whose wife Esther, when their kid died of meningitis at the age of three, developed chronic depression that, on good days, found her curled up on their closet floor. Yitzy, who flailed. There was Mookie, whose kid sister Serafina, a simple girl who worked as a maid, got pregnant at sixteen and stepped off the platform at Bleecker Street into the path of the express train. Mookie, who switched ropes mid-air. There was Donny G, who was incinerated in a tank during Desert Storm. There was Paolo, sterile from mumps at the age of nine because — until that happened — Polly Angelotta did not believe in childhood inoculations. There was Tess, who couldn't commit to any man. There was Catherine Coleman, who could. And there was me, who would die one day over a flower shop on Macdougal Street, laid out by Tess in a shroud made of felafel wrappers.

Standing in the dark at my window I knew I'd get Catherine Coleman's blackmailer, but I was never very good at following directions. She had taken as a lover a man whose mind was clearly on something other than his dying, needlepointing wife. There was no way in hell I wasn't going to bother Hugo Kilcannon.

Across the street the Miller's High Life sign went black.

WAVERLY ACADEMY OCCUPIES A SERIES OF BROWNSTONES NEAR WASHINGTON Square Park. Founded in 1912 by Adelaide Temple Waverly who apparently had nothing better to do with her money, it was dedicated to the intellectual advancement of young men who wanted to get into an Ivy League school and to get laid, preferably not in that order. Not all of this information appears on the bronze plaque alongside the front door. I made up the part about intellectual advancement.

For the occasion I borrowed one of Paolo's Armani rip-off suits, with the single-breasted jacket and pleated pants. I gelled my hair, wondered if it was too late to get an ear pierced, then washed out the gel and went on my way. I caught Hugo Kilcannon on his way to teach a squash class. For a forty-seven-year-old adulterer whose wife was dying, he was impressive. Hugo's hair stayed back without gel, mousse or threats. It was well-bred hair. All the rest of him was in Ralph Lauren whites. We walked together down tiled corridors, past walls covered with student art, past trophy cases, to a new wing invisible from the street. The four million dollar Vandevere Athletic Wing. It was a spa for adolescent boys who could lift, step, sweat, soak and steam all in one convenient downtown location.

Kilcannon had a sleek ease I would have envied if he hadn't also had Catherine Coleman. No eye bags, no cheek stubble, no ear tufts, no uncorrected nose bumps.

He was a pen and ink drawing, all painstaking lines and tawny monochrome. I stuffed my fists in my borrowed fake Armani pockets and tried not to blister the bonkmaster's skin with all the hostility I was radiating. He asked my purpose. I told him I represented the interests of Catherine Coleman.

"Catherine Coleman," he repeated. "Ah, yes."

"She's being bothered."

"Bothered?"

"By letters."

"Bothersome letters," he said, putting it all together. Three young men headed toward us from the lockers, naked except for the white gym towels tucked at their waists. "Are you saying someone's harassing Catherine Coleman?"

"You could say that." My tactic, going in, was to be oblique. Keep it vague what exactly Catherine Coleman had hired me to do. Rely on the other guy's powers of inference, including the blackmailer's.

The young men stopped long enough at the door to the steam room for Hugo Kilcannon to make introductions. The brawny redhead was Will DeRee, of the Newport DeRees. The bottle blond with a swimmer's long torso was Perry Vandevere, of the Athletic Wing Vandeveres. The third was Dexter Kilcannon, the bonkmaster's son. Slighter than the other two, he had a smile that could grind diamond to dust.

"Dad?" The playful DeRee kid tried to get the towel off the waist of Dexter. What could be better in this whole lopsided world than to be seventeen and sweaty and rich?

"Dex?"

"Something happen to Ms Coleman?"

"That's what Mr Angelotta's here to tell us." I saw it then, complete, and I didn't know what to do with it: to Hugo Kilcannon, I wasn't here to get information, I was here to impart it. Where, did he think, was the money in that?

"Is she being stalked?" The horror on the face of the Vandevere boy was tweaked.

"In a manner of — "

Kilcannon's hand was splayed on my shoulder. "Do you take steam?"

"What?"

"The steam bath, Mr Angelotta."

"Sure."

"Feel free."

"Now? Here?"

"The boys will set you up. I'm sorry to hear about Catherine's trouble, but I've got a class to teach." I'd been dumped. But dumped classy. Maybe he'd learned it from Catherine. The DeRee kid, who outweighed me by twenty pounds, showed me to a locker, tossed me a clean towel, and had the good grace to turn his back while I stripped, wondering how the hell these boarding school boys had co-opted my agenda. Five minutes later I joined the others in the steam room, stumbling over Dexter's feet on my way to a higher bench. So what if heat rises? It gave me an edge to look down on them, although the atmosphere was a throw-back to the time when no-damn-body was around to witness what marvels were brought out of the steam. Out of this steam could come only three naked seventeen-year-olds, marvels in their own right. One of them pulled a chain and we all disappeared in a surge of steam. The chain clinked.

"Nice woman, Ms Coleman."

"Dex knew her the best."

"I wouldn't say that." On the bench below me, Dexter sat up, resting his elbows on his knees.

We steamed on, these lads and I, for about half an hour, and while they regaled me with how DeRee was rowing for Yale in the fall, and Vandevere was debating for Dartmouth, I swear I could feel my molecular structure changing. Dex said he was heading for Princeton, and everybody got real quiet, including me, who didn't know what anything meant. "Dex," Vandevere explained, "has been going to Princeton since he was in the third grade."

"So Princeton's old, old ass-wipe news," DeRee added, "and we're all just tired of it."

"Except for me," Dex said, and through the steam I could see that smile.

They listened while I told them about Angelotta Investigations, Tess's book shop, Mookie's Novelties, and even Bunny Burgoyne. They whooped and tossed my towel around. Then they whispered a few confidences about favorite females. Vandevere mentioned the lunch lady's easy daughter. "Oh, like you know," DeRee laughed, and offered up a mysterious street girl named Liu who, for a fair price, supplemented her income from second-rate bead work with first-rate hand jobs. "Like you know," Dex laughed.

"You only hear," Vandevere scoffed.

"Hear, my ass, Van. I — " he said archly for the full effect " — do."

"Do, my ass, Will."

"Wouldn't you just love me to?"

And they all roared.

TWO PHONE CALLS, BOTH BAD. I MADE THE MISTAKE OF CALLING MY MOTHER AND telling her how I spent the morning, then had to listen to her berate me for ten minutes about what steam baths do to a guy's sperm count. Ever since the problem with Paolo, she had taken an abnormal interest in my reproductive health. The second call I made to Catherine Coleman at work, who picked up on the second ring and just stated her name. First I told her the part she wouldn't like, since I figured I'd move quickly to the boys, where I'd redeem myself. "I talked to Kil-cannon, and he — "

"To Hugo?" She was aggrieved. "I told you not to — "

"All the more reason."

"Do you always do what you damn well please?"

"No." Otherwise my lips would be exploring her hair.

She raised her voice. "I specifically told you — "

"Catherine — Ms Coleman — you may feel like eight shades of shit for sleeping with him, but at present you are the victim of a crime and it's entirely likely the Kilcannon guy has some information."

Apparently I had lost my powers of persuasion. "I should fire you."

"So fire me."

"You're fired."

"Fine. What are you doing tomorrow night?"

She sucked in air. "Are you making a date?"

There it was. "Yes."

"I'm a client." Her shock was boundless.

"Former," I reminded her. "I figure over dinner and a few drinks we could map out how — at the present rate of extortion — you can pay your blackmailer well over half a million dollars for the next ten years. Maybe you could set up a trust."

Silence. Then: "You're back on the case."

"My fees have increased since the last time I worked for you."

She hung up. I laughed myself over to the fridge where I got a beer, which I uncapped and raised to the absent Catherine.

I SPENT A JUNE AFTERNOON ANY FOOL COULD TELL YOU IS PUT TO BETTER USE FLY fishing chasing down the other names on Catherine Coleman's list. There was the retired librarian from the academy, the varsity tennis coach, the dorm housekeeper, and two of Catherine Coleman's neighbors at One Sheridan Square. I took a chance scratching off the names of five Waverly boys who had graduated over the last year and gone away to colleges that ruled out Manhattan postmarks. What Kilcannon had summed up as "bothersome letters" was how I packaged Catherine Coleman's problem. By dinner time I had concluded that the house-keeper seemed cagey and that another shot at Hugo Kilcannon would just about restore my sperm count. As I changed into a cooler pair of drawstring pants and a loose shirt, I thought about DeRee and his pals. I had thirteen years on them. Less tread on my tires. Even so — as I dug out a pair of sandals, remembering their rich boys' act — it was good to know that steaming me wasn't quite the same as snowing me.

TESS MANAGED A MYSTERY BOOK SHOP ON MACDOUGAL STREET CALLED MIND Over Murder. Her boss, who had to be ninety, had owned an electrical contracting company on Long Island back in the fifties when Levittown was built, and retired at forty a rich man. The book shop was an amusement he rarely visited from any of his homes on Cape Cod, Hilton Head, or the Isle of Wight. Eight years ago he had given Tess the key, the records, and instructions to keep it afloat and bother him only in the event of total loss by fire. Tess wrote her own paychecks, sold what she liked, and kept her own hours. When I went in she looked up from the stool where she sat at the front counter, the hair around her forehead kinking up in the humidity the way it had for the past twenty years since her part of the family had moved to the Village and I met her. Overhead the ceiling fans circled in a kind of mechanical torpor.

About the time Tess and I hit our twenties something impenetrable dropped into our friendship. We went from sharing our first dates, hangovers, heartbreaks, and general life gripes, to telling each other everything except word one on the subject of love affairs. For that we got an intermediary: Mookie. Tess had clammed up first, making me wonder whether that side of her life was too hectic to recount, but when I ran it by Mookie he said no, so I concluded I was not the sort of guy Tess trusted with the information. It hurt. So I took her lead and kept women out of our conversation, but there wasn't a time it didn't feel false.

"Mookie tells me you're in love." Tess turned her dark eyes my way, dog earing a page in *Publisher's Weekly* and setting it aside.

I leaned on the counter, pushed the coins around in the dish with the sign NEED A PENNY — TAKE A PENNY. Browsing part way down the aisle in Forties Classics were an old couple in matching Bermuda shorts. For no reason at all I felt like a fool. "Is that what Mookie said?"

She smiled. "Isn't that what you told him?"

"It's what I said," I looked at Tess, brushing a loose eyelash from her cheek. My thumb made two more soft swipes after I had already seen the eyelash fall off, which I failed to mention to Tess. She was motionless in the heat. Her top was white linen. She watched me without speaking, the hairs on her arms light from lying out on her rooftop. She was Tess. Her top was white. My mouth felt dry. No one in my life was more present than Tess, or more remote.

I didn't tell Tess much about Catherine Coleman because Catherine was a client — and because it violated the role of Mookie in this part of our lives — and when it came right down to it I didn't have anything to tell. When I finished she made a strange comment, telling me I took people at face value, but she gave me a fond look when she said it, and slid off the stool, heading for the Bermuda shorts, who were dropping books and bickering over whether EC Bentley was out of print.

The door to the shop opened and in walked Perry Vandevere and Dexter Kilcannon in Hawaiian print shirts. If they hadn't looked so sincere I'd have said they were slumming here on Macdougal Street, dropping some cash, getting carded at Umberto's, soaking up the funk. American royalty in tropical disguise. The three of us shuffled around each other for a while, laughing like old buds, and Dexter loped off down one of the aisles labeled Cheap Thrills. Vandevere called after him not to spend all his scholarship money, then grinned at me and added that Dex was getting pretty nearly a free ride at Princeton in the fall, which was a damn good thing since Kilcannon père had only his — here the boy reached hard for the concept — job, no investments, no college funds, no — Vandevere's upturned hand flicked open and shut — resources.

They had been to my place, looking for me, and on the way down to Tess's stopped in Mookie's Novelties, Casbah Jewelry, and Shlomo's Shawarmas. Half an hour later Dexter walked out of Mind Over Murder with a signed first edition of a James M Cain with a lurid paper jacket he couldn't believe he found. Vandevere put the purchase on his platinum Visa while the Kilcannon boy thumbed through the book, murmuring he'd pay him back. I took them to Umberto's and sat at one of the sidewalk tables with Dexter while Vandevere went inside to spring for three espressos. I felt peculiar having a high school senior boy buying me so much as a cup of coffee, but for Dex it wasn't an issue. Who spent, and who got spent on, was elevated to a kind of etiquette.

Adrian, Umberto's bouncer who's missing both his eyebrows and half his jaw, showed up as he sometimes does well before his shift with his ring-tailed monkey, Chuckie, dressed in an embroidered vest and a disposable diaper, who delighted Dexter Kilcannon. Slip Chuckie two bits, he pockets it. A buck, he kisses your hand. Nobody wanted to know what Chuckie would do for a five. I floated Dexter two bucks — one for each hand — and sat back in my metal chair while Adrian let Chuckie climb, chittering, on Dexter's shoulder.

He was someone who made you want to please him. To lay offerings at his feet. Women would be vying to add carnal knowledge to Dexter Kilcannon's course load. I watched him bend his head, laughing, while Chuckie skittered across the back of his neck, stopping long enough to tug, with a look of amazement, at Dex's hair. Even the monkey got it. Dexter turned his face to what was left of the sun, and I saw in him the same sloping jaw line and tawny skin his father still had thirty years later. Tiny beauty marks like sign posts made a tour of his face — you'd swear it was the first face in all of creation — above his lip, on his cheeks, near the corners of his eyes. Chuckie slung himself around to Dexter's chest, stepped up to the table's edge, turned to face him, and reached up solemnly with both brown paws to cup the young man's chin. "Ah, Chuckie," Dex said softly to the uncomprehending monkey, "now you pay me."

THE WIND PICKED UP, LIFTING STREET TRASH, CRUMPLED NAPKINS, PLASTIC EMPTIES, sending them scattering before the rest of us even realized the day was changing. I was alone at the table — the Waverly boys said they'd be back later that night with DeRee — staring into the fine black sludge at the bottom of my cup. When Vandevere had come back outside, Devi, one of Umberto's servers, came just ahead of him, the coffee on a small tray. She was a beautiful woman with choppy hair and wide-set hazel eyes that settled on each of us. Vandevere, whose experience of women consisted of centerfolds and the rumpus room between his ears, was clogged with the kind of unschooled stuttering excitement that only the presence of a beautiful female can provide. And then there was Dexter. He took in Devi with the appreciative detachment of a man who felt no strangeness in the company of women because he had held the mystery in his hands. Soft whispering skirts had been set aside for him. It was a shrewd and comprehensive look the seventeen-year-old gave the server nearly twice his age — the skin under his eyes tightened as he took her in. A glance told her he knew where she liked to be touched and what she liked to be told. Hell, even I didn't know that.

Despite what Perry Vandevere said about the lunch lady's easy daughter, I would bet Chuckie's vest he was a virgin. Dexter Kilcannon — I pushed aside my cup — Dexter Kilcannon was not. There were times, Tess, I wanted to tell her, that face value is the best value. Make no mistake. I checked my watch: ten to five. Pushing myself away from the table, I walked with no particular haste across the street to Angelotta Investigations, where I placed a call to New Jersey.

IN THE BACK ROOM OF MY APARTMENT, I HAVE A PRETTY DECENT SOUND SYSTEM, one leather chair that cups you like an astronaut, a Turkish rug and that's it. There have been women who have tried to add plants and pictures — not to mention themselves — but nothing beats the way it is. The window to the old Angelotta fire escape was wide open. Rain drummed the dirty metal platform, wind rushed the sheer curtains at me, where I sat in the near dark listening to an old Phoebe Snow CD. Earlier I made myself eat the tabouli Mookie brought over. I even took a little Chianti, courtesy of Tess. Nobody talked much. Somebody turned on a lamp. I had swept the front room. Changed the sheets on the futon, imagining myself consoling Catherine Coleman in a way that would drive the treacherous Dexter — blackmailing her with the knowledge of her affair with his father — from her consciousness for a few hours. I had come to manhood believing that passion was a defense that stilled the sorrowing mind and kept death outside the striving flesh. I checked for my revolver, which I dropped, disgusted, back into the desk drawer.

Tess cleared the dishes. They knew Catherine Coleman was coming at eleven. They knew the case was ending, but that was all. Tess crouched beside me, suddenly, but finding nothing to say, left without a word. Mookie followed. Maybe in a few weeks I could tell them how the financial aid office at Princeton told the Mr Angelotta from Waverly Academy's counseling department that they had made their financial aid decision months ago about Dexter Kilcannon: they couldn't support his acceptance with any scholarship money. There were students with stronger academic records and greater need. When I passed the information on to my client over the phone, her voice shriveled up, and all I heard her say was "Dex," spoken in something other than disbelief. When I told her he, Vandevere and DeRee would be on Macdougal Street around eleven, no, she said, she didn't want a conference with him, she didn't want the cops, she didn't even want the money back. It seemed to me she wanted her mind stripped back to some point pre-Kilcannon. But there was going to be a meeting, whether she liked it or not.

BY HALF-PAST ELEVEN I KNEW SHE WASN'T GOING TO SHOW, AND I HAD TO GET OUT on the street and walk around, rain or no rain, or pretty soon I'd cut myself on my own edginess. I was pulling on a flannel shirt when the screaming started. A woman. Somewhere close. I was out the door just in time to see one of the Asian kitchen workers at Umberto's back out of the alley, still screaming. Adrian came bolting out of the restaurant, but I got to her first. She was slippery with panic, pointing, twisting to get away. I handed her off to Adrian and ran farther into the alley, past the garbage cans, to where delivery crates were stacked, the smell of wet wood mixing with city pavement and death.

Someone was sprawled in the dark on his back, hardly lit by the blue bulb over Umberto's back door. At the sight of the Hawaiian print shirt my stomach lurched clear out of my body. It was Dexter Kilcannon. The entire front of the boy was soaked with blood. Oh, Christ. "9-1-1," I yelled, choking, to the shadows behind me. I flung myself at him, grabbing his shoulders. My hand touched the sliced shirt where a knife had gone in near his heart. "Call 9-1-1." I felt for a carotid pulse. None. Feet pounded behind me. I looked up to see DeRee and Vandevere push their way past a few people. When they saw Dexter, DeRee lunged. "Oh, my God, oh, shit." Vandevere grabbed him and they both started sobbing, filling the little alley on Macdougal Street with the pain even money couldn't fix.

Tess got through the crowd. "Carm?"

"Just take them," I said, stepping back while DeRee threw up, pushing the sobbing boys toward her. "Just get them out of here." Adrian worked on dispersing the crowd. I turned back to the Kilcannon boy, my hand pulling at my hair, praying for the sirens that would end it.

"Let me through."

"Lady — "

"Let me through!"

Catherine Coleman.

I staggered to my feet, nearly down for the count, my brain overturned in the blue light. She looked at me only quickly, then past me, and I will never forget her shriek. It was the sound of torment from some other place altogether than this damn world, where people play checkers and Eli Whitney invented the cotton gin.

"Dex!" She pushed me aside and fell on the dead boy. "Dex." Catherine Coleman didn't have enough arms to hold him or enough breath to bring him back. "Dex, oh God, oh honey," I watched her cry into his hair, bloody his face with her useless, tainted hands, croon to his corpse while she rocked. And in a rift of understanding that slices wounds of its own, I suddenly saw which Kilcannon, two years ago when he was only fifteen, had been her lover.

THE RAIN WAS LETTING UP. I SAT ALONE FOR TWO HOURS IN WASHINGTON SQUARE Park, heaped on a bench. Nobody bothered me. Nobody bothers a man with acres of fresh bloodstains on his face and hands and clothes. Those set me apart. Even by Village standards. By the time I pushed myself off the bench at nearly two in the morning, the raindrops had become the kind of mist that bursts on your skin and floats white and graceful in the street light. I headed home to Macdougal Street, where beautiful errant boys bleed out their lives in unfamiliar alleys. Some time tomorrow — if the cops didn't fill my dance card — I'd go to Shlomo's Shawarmas and see if his brother in Atlantic City could use some help at his fried dough stand on the boardwalk. Let Paolo hire some real help for the night shift. Turn the key forever on Angelotta Investigations.

I remembered how she had come out of the alley, Catherine Coleman, while the EMS team worked on him, her hair flat with blood and rain. She stood there, two feet away from me, her arms hanging. Her lips swollen with tears and un-responsive kisses. The half-circle of gawkers curved out into the street. I had seen people like Catherine Coleman before, people walking, bloody, away from wrecks. Car wrecks, bomb wrecks, election night results. She was in shock and I didn't give any sort of a damn. When she turned to look at me, all of her turned, as if her joints had fused into one brittle and inflexible bone. Her mouth was open. Through the sound of the rain I realized she was crying, a shrill line of pain that seemed disconnected from her eyes. She started to raise her arms toward me. My hands flew up, hard, and I stepped back. "No matter what you think it was," I said just loud enough for her to hear, "the state of New York calls it rape."

No wonder she only wanted the name.

No wonder she didn't want the cops.

I had given her the name. The question was: had I given her, too, the boy's life? Had I set him up on Macdougal Street for his own murder? On the phone I had insisted that she come at eleven when the Kilcannon boy and his friends were going to be doing a late-night shop crawl. When Vandevere stopped sobbing inside Umberto's, where Yitzy fixed them up with coffee and sandwiches, he told me that the three of them had split up. He and DeRee wanted to check out a Third World music store, and Dexter wanted to revisit a couple of places he'd already been earlier that day. Was Catherine Coleman capable of stabbing him and then grieving for him? End the blackmail he had going for himself to pay the bills at Princeton. End the threat of his exposing her crime. Her own crime. It's one thing had she been a player in an adultery gig, the blind she used on me about Hugo Kilcannon — it was something else again to be charged with the statutory rape of a boy half her age.

When I hit Macdougal Street Mr Bello, the insomniac baker, was sweeping outside his shop. "So there's trouble down at your end," he said, glancing at me. "There's trouble everywhere," I told him, and he snorted. As I got to my door, I saw on the other side of the street the yellow police tape strung across Umberto's alley. I didn't stop. Upstairs I threw my bloodstained clothes into the bathtub and showered until the hot water ran out.

When I got up at half past seven and threw on enough clothes to go down the block for some coffee without getting arrested, I found a note from Mookie stuck in my door. *Carm, I have info, come ASAP.* Coffee will always beat info. Twenty minutes later, I stopped at Novelties long enough to see it was locked and deserted, and went upstairs to the Mendez place. Mookie struck me as stiff, but I wasn't accustomed to seeing him ambulatory much before the shop opened at eleven. I was waiting for whatever urgent info he wanted to impart, but I knew Mookie did things in his own time, so when he raised the window to the fire escape, I went first. Anything, I figured, was better than letting my brain trail back to the crimes of Catherine Coleman. I saw the rope first thing. After a minute, while I stood on the Mendez fire escape, where I hadn't been for years, Mookie came out. His smile was strange. "There's something from the shop I want to give you," he said, "later." His head jerked. "Just inside, okay?"

"Okay."

We stood with our arms folded overlooking the courtyard, where someone had again put petunias in the toilet planter. The sky was a fresh blue, the few stark clouds shapely and unmoving. Someone's talk radio drifted up to us. Somewhere else a baby fussed. It was hard to tell it had rained. It was hard to tell whether it would ever rain again. Mookie had rigged up the rope to his railing, just as his crazy dad had done, and it lay coiled at our feet. Serafina, he said, was seventeen when she died — seventeen and four months pregnant. He uncoiled the rope slowly, still talking. She had quit school a while before and found a job in housekeeping.

"Some hotel," I offered.

"No, no hotel. A boarding school just a few blocks from here. Waverly Academy."

When it happened, he got a call to come identify her body. Mookie shuddered, staring at nothing. He had nothing to go on, no name. Serafina wouldn't give up the name of the one who had done it to her. But he recalled how once, when she had first started working there, she went around singing about the one with dots, or spots, on his face, and when she could tell Mookie didn't want to hear about it, she stopped.

Mookie stood up, holding the rope. There was no loop this time. There would be no tricks. My breath was shallow. I prayed for sudden total deafness so I wouldn't have to hear. Still the baby fussed. Still Mookie spoke. "After she — " his mouth twitched " — died, I went to the school looking for him. Looking for the one with dots. With pimples, I thought Serafina had meant." He shrugged. "There were so many it was hopeless."

Then yesterday three boys came into his shop from Waverly Academy. And he saw right away what had charmed Serafina. Mookie handed me the rope, then jerked his head over the side. "Go on, Carm." His eyes were on mine. What had been reckless joy at twelve had changed into terror at thirty. It was all I could do not to check the knot, but I couldn't have Mookie see my eyes lower. "Go on." While I swung I wouldn't have to hear him, he would shut up, he would tell me he was just kidding. He would be Mookie Mendez again, twelve forever, the best on the ropes, king of the switcheroo, pride of the Basques, leader of the Macdougal Street Strays. I swung out, felt the old freedom, felt lighter than the shadow of rain water left behind, my heart filled with all the years in between freedom and death. I flailed like Yitzy, I latched my knees over the railing like Donny G, I was elegant like Paolo, and with a sob, I spreadeagled one last time for Mookie Mendez, whose knot held.

He grabbed me, solemn, and helped me back over the railing, nodding. Then he kneaded my shoulder. *Ain't nobody a better friend than you.* "Just to be sure," he said softly, taking the rope in his own hands, "I asked him if he remembered a little maid called Serafina." He did — he was the only one of them who did — and while he was looking at the penny postcards he said he wondered whatever happened to her. When the dot boy showed up again alone, Mookie closed the shop like a new pal and with his arm on the boy's shoulder walked him to Umberto's for an espresso. "In the alley," Mookie said, "I told him about Serafina."

"Mook, no," I cried as he sprang over the railing with the rope in hand and swung out. The years flew up in a shock of morning sunlight, and he was for that moment more heartbreakingly beautiful than Dexter Kilcannon. "Mookie, no," I shouted, trying to grab him, failing, as he swung out again, jerking around to face me, our eyes the rope that spanned all years to come, and I watched him as he reached the middle of the arc and with calm deliberation, let go.

WHAT MOOKIE HAD GIVEN ME FROM THE SHOP WAS WRAPPED IN A HAND TOWEL and masking tape. It was one of the naked lady letter openers, crusted nearly to the hilt with the dead boy's blood. I presented it to the cops and started living on my fire escape. My clothes smelled like sweat. My hair was uncombed. Sometimes I crawled inside to the john. Sometimes Paolo left food. I smelled old Mrs Schreiber's chulent on the stove, I learned the times of day the Cooperman baby fussed, I heard the lady on the first floor tug at the squeaky clothesline. At night I wrapped myself in a thin blanket and stared at the stars, drifting. By late afternoon one day I took off my shirt and sat against the brick wall with my head tucked into my bent knees.

There was a knock at the glass of the raised window. I twisted my head just enough to see Tess climb out beside me. We sat in silence for a while, and I didn't know what she could say or do to bring me back, so I stared at a scar on my ankle. Finally, she spoke. "You look like a kid swinging upside down on a rope," she said, her voice tight with feeling, "and your leg's coming through." My chest felt like it cracked with the memory. The face I turned to her must have been awful, and I couldn't raise my lips higher than my arm. "So pull me in," I said, and my arms went up around her neck as she grabbed me and held on tight. With my head on her breast, against skin that for no good reason I felt I had known forever, I lay half-curled against her, until nightfall.

the fear

jason gould

Born in 1971, Jason Gould lives in Hull in the north of England and works in web design. He has had a number of short stories published in a variety of magazines and anthologies, with work forthcoming in Beneath the Ground (edited by Joel Lane) and The Year's Best Dark Fantasy (edited by Steve Savile). Jason is currently at work on several new short stories.

HE CALLS AT TEN AFTER SIX. SHE WANTS TO LET IT RING SO HE WON'T KNOW SHE'S BEEN sitting by the phone all afternoon but it's impossible and she picks it up right away.

"Hello?"

"Hi."

"Just arrived?"

"Five minutes ago."

"Nice hotel?"

"Very nice," he says. Then softly, "But nicer if you were here."

"Really?"

"Of course. I'm incomplete without you."

She gathers in breath, says, "I'm missing you, too."

"It's only three days," he points out. "I'll be back by your side before you can say 'Papa Bear'."

"Papa Bear!"

He emits the noise people emit at a dewy-eyed puppy waddling in rolls of fat.

"I can hear bells," she says.

"There's a church across the road. I'll be needing my earplugs tonight."

"Oh I miss you!" she says. "Damn conference!"

"Damn conference!"

"Will you call me later?"

"Try to stop me."

"At bedtime?"

"About ten. Early night tonight. Big day tomorrow."

"You'd better unpack," she says.

"I'll talk to you soon."

"I love you, Papa Bear," she says. "You're the best thing that's happened to me. You make me glad for divorce courts."

"I love you too," he says.

"Bye."

"Bye."

After he's hung up she holds the receiver to her chest as if it were the favourite soft toy of a missing child. When she feels able she eases it on to the hook and goes upstairs to shower. She sings Lionel Richie, Barry White etc beneath the water, folding into the lyrics his name. She flutters heavenly in the steam. Then she takes the telephone to bed where she awaits its ring, laying on her belly in pink pyjamas kicking her legs: the prospective housewife in some 1950s Government guidance film.

HE CALLS WHEN HE'S ABOUT TO TURN IN FOR THE NIGHT. HE'S IN BED DRINKING cocoa, he says, and he's brewed a cup for her — thick and creamy with lots of sugar, just how she likes it — which he's placed with a digestive biscuit by the phone.

"I wish I were there to drink it," she says.

"So do I."

"How's the room?"

"Empty without you."

"The bed?"

"Huge. And cold."

"Same here."

"I'll soon be back. And then I'll keep you warm. Forever."

"Forever?"

"Yes," he says, "forever."

"Being on my own was horrible," she says. "I never want to be alone again."

"You won't. I will always be with you."

She sniffs, coughs. Sniffs again.

"The hotel's probably charging a fortune for these calls, so perhaps best if I say goodnight."

"Oh," she says, at odds to keep disappointment from her voice. "Oh, OK."

"I'll call tomorrow."

"All right. You know," she adds, "now we've spent some time apart, I feel as if I know Papa Bear better."

"I love you," he says.

"And I love you," she replies.

Goodnight is said four times. At last he puts down his phone, though she clutches hers to her bosom like she did earlier only this time more tightly, as if the missing child had been found dead and deflowered in a ditch.

"HELLO . . . ? HELLO . . . ? ARE YOU STILL THERE? YOU HAVEN'T PUT THE PHONE down properly. Can you hear me?"

She waits to see if he'll notice. He doesn't and she hollers into the mouthpiece, causing it to vibrate. He obviously hasn't heard so she attempts to cut the line from her end by putting down the receiver and then picking it back up. She does this several times. The connection stays open.

She decides to forget about it and go to sleep (all it means is she'll be unable to generate or receive calls) when she realises she can hear him moving about: floor creaking, drawers sliding in and out, bed squeaking. She may as well be standing with her hands over her eyes in the corner of the room. If he drifts off to sleep and snores that oh so cute snore she will simply have to rush out of the house and take the first train to The Travel Tavern, 144 Euston Road, London NW1 2AU. Or stay up all night enchanted by the purr in her ear.

For a minute the room is silent and she wonders if the operator has intervened. But then she hears a low knock. Body weight releases from the bed. An indeterminate exchange follows at the door. Someone laughs, then the door scrapes across the carpet, shutting heavily. She hears him say, "Sit down." And, "Not there, there." And, "Would you like a drink?"

A voice — quiet and male, dry and subdued and splintering at the higher notes — asks for a glass of water.

"The tumbler in the bathroom is broken," he says. "Would you like this bottle of Evian?"

"OK."

The bed groans as someone gets comfortable.

"Do you mind if I sit here?" says Papa Bear.

"It's your room."

"Only until the morning." A pause. Then he says: "Let me look at you." Silence, for a second. Then: "Not bad, not bad. You should use a moisturiser. And you have a few blackheads on your brow. But I quite like that. How old are you?"

"Eighteen."

"Eighteen? Not much on you for eighteen."

"I'm not a big fan of food."

"What *are* you a big fan of?"

"Cocks," says the lad, "and come, and having my backside smacked."

"I bet you are," he says, a click in his voice like a limpet releasing itself from a rock. "I can see in your eyes you're a real slut-boy."

Blinking quickly, she removes the telephone from her ear to stare at it bewildered. She'd thought the visitor would be associated with a) the hotel, or b) the following day's conference. Room service perhaps, so sorry to disturb at such a late hour; or final preparation for Kitchens 2001. And if she were to go immediately to sleep she might still believe that come the morning. But if she did, would she ever be able to look at him again without hearing in her head what she'd just heard him say?

Or *thought* she'd heard him say, because of course it might be a crossed line. It resembled his voice, but was it? London was a fair old way; there was ample opportunity for interference. She traces the cord from the handset to the wall as if any malfunction might show up in the wire. She's ready to check the telephone directory for technical advice when she realises a crossed line would be impossible: in the background the church over the road had been striking eleven.

Like a psychic with a seashell, afraid to hear the scream of the drowned, she draws the receiver to the side of her head — ". . . kiss your arse, and your thin hard prick . . ." — and pulls it quickly away to lay it carefully and reverentially down on the bed, too far for what's being said to be heard but near enough to keep an eye on while she decides what to do.

SHE SITS AND THINKS, SIPPING EVERY SO OFTEN AT A GLASS OF WATER.

First she's confident it's a hoax, with or without her boyfriend's consent, and that she and he will look back and smile; then she decides a satellite station is running an adult movie and he's tuned in by mistake; then she thinks maybe he and a neighbouring resident (Atkins perhaps, who is also there for Kitchens 2001, and who is openly gay) have their wires jumbled and all this same sex shenanigans is going on the other side of the wall; and then she thinks this, or this, or this. And each explanation is in its own way believable. But it's a transitory belief and in turn each scenario — like the stupid invention it is — falls flat on its face. Before long all the innocent solutions have expired.

He has a secret life, she decides next. Not a secret life in which he participates in buggery, but a secret life in which he's a back-slapping Sweeneyesque plain-clothes cop assigned to vice. Nauseated by the filth through which he is forced to wade day after day, he conceals his true profession from those for whom he cares by masquerading as Babylon Kitchen's Head Salesman. This she likes. A picture forms: he stands at the peeling window frame of some North London tenement gazing out at the sunrise and dreaming of her, while behind him three partly dressed women, a teenage lad and an overweight Turk in an okra-stained vest argue with the arresting officer. She adores the duteousness in his eyes, the chivalry in his manner as he drapes his raincoat round the nearest call-girl. But just as she's beginning to be at home in the image it veers for the worse and, sending everyone out of the room, he stands the boy on a chair and tugs down his underpants. She flicks it away.

Perhaps the strangest idea to pass her way tonight is that the man with whom she is in love has battled all his life a latent homosexuality, and — now he's fallen for her — he feels compelled to realise the fantasy once and for all before asking her place at the altar. In this she thinks how he might kiss the lad — an effeminate, borderline transsexual — but then throw up down the side of the bed. Cleaning his lips with a tissue he tosses some cash on the pillow and, saying he's made a terrible mistake, asks the caller to leave. When he's alone he brushes his teeth vigorously, rinses his mouth and then phones and tells her over and over, lump in throat, how he is so utterly devoted.

Could she handle this? Yes, she thinks; yes, she could. It almost had a nobility about it, in that he was attending to those aspects of his life he felt were a threat to their future happiness. How many other men were so in tune with their hearts; so thoughtful? Maybe she was lucky.

But if she didn't have a problem with that, why did she then have a problem with the truth? Why was it so hard to accept that the only person in the world for whom she gave a shit was attracted sexually to men?

Or *could* she handle it? Flesh is flesh, after all; a rut is a rut. It wasn't as if he and this kid were in love. It was more as if he were engaging in an act necessary for his life to function. In actual fact it wasn't that different to taking a drink on a Friday evening or jetting off to a Spanish beach for ten days in August. It was a counterbalance. It meant nothing. And better this than he floundering over the edge, Uzi-ing families in Burger King for want of a male tongue on his dick.

So she thinks: did I overreact? She thinks: if not losing him rests upon him ploughing the occasional rent-boy, then is that so bad? It wasn't abnormal. Hell, she'd seen the chat shows: 'My Guy Fancies Other Guys!'; 'I Scrub Lavatories To Pay My Boyfriend's Butt-Buddies!'; 'I Saw My Guy Kissing Santa!'. She was in good company. And it *was* a new millennium. And she wasn't old-fashioned.

FEELING MORE LIBERAL, SHE RETURNS TO THE PHONE. SHE CAN'T MAKE ANYTHING out until she holds the receiver hard against her ear, and then she is able to identify certain sounds: the steady *yunk-yunk-yunk* of bodies shunting in rhythm; the suck and unsuck of skin on skin; a dry gassy sound expelled from a throat every fourth second.

She breathes in, holds down tears. There is a world of difference between this and how she imagined two men having a fuck might sound. Her sole experience in the area was years ago when a friend had entertained a hen party with a gay porn film. But that had been all 'ream out my ass', 'choke on my dick', 'drink my hot come'. She wished for such stage-managed phrases now; the way it was — with neither he nor his date speaking, with the occasional terse inhalation when some especially tender zone was touched — it seemed too real: more akin to genuine lovemaking than a meaningless screw with a meaningless lover in an equally meaningless hotel.

Fearful of the motive behind the fuck, she listens more closely by plugging her non-telephone ear. She dreads the faintest proclamation of love. At the least she expects to hear an 'I love you' mumbled in passion from somewhere between the sheets. But for many minutes there is nothing bar those noises which attend any act of vigorous intercourse. And then her breath halts, because on the other end

THE FEAR

68

of the wire at the other end of the country the bed and the bodies are suddenly still, and the lad is asking, "Why have you stopped? What's wrong? Don't you like me?"

And she's thinking, my God, he's about to tell him he loves him. My God, he's about to say, 'I love you. Be mine. Come away with me.'

My God, she thinks, I love a man who loves a man.

She listens. And this is what she hears:

SLUT-BOY: Why have you stopped? What's wrong? Don't you like me?

PAPA BEAR: On the contrary. I like you very much. But you were about to come.

SLUT-BOY: And . . . ?

PAPA BEAR: And it's too soon for you to come.

SLUT-BOY: But I need to!

PAPA BEAR: Whose money is it?

SLUT-BOY: Yours.

PAPA BEAR: Then you come when I say. Not before. OK?

SLUT-BOY: OK. I suppose. So . . . what now?

PAPA BEAR: Something juicy. Something really juicy.

SLUT-BOY: Yeah?

PAPA BEAR: I want to give you the best orgasm of your life.

SLUT-BOY (SARCASTICALLY): Oh, really?

PAPA BEAR: No bullshit. This will take your tits off. You won't have felt anything like this before.

SLUT-BOY: I'm not doing drugs.

PAPA BEAR: No drugs.

SLUT-BOY: You're not peeing on me.

PAPA BEAR: Wouldn't dream of it.

SLUT-BOY: Then, what?

PAPA BEAR: Turn over. Lay flat on your stomach.

THE BED SQUEAKS

SLUT-BOY: I see you took the phone off the hook.

PAPA BEAR: I did?

SLUT-BOY: I guess I really am in for a good time.

PAPA BEAR: You bet.

SLUT-BOY: Hey, what you doing up there?

PAPA BEAR: Ignore me. Pretend I'm not here.

SLUT-BOY: You gonna jack into my hair? I know an accountant who gets off on that.

PAPA BEAR: Nothing like that. I'm just going to sit up here on your back for a while. Be good and maybe later I'll ejaculate in your mouth.

SLUT-BOY: Promise?

PAPA BEAR: I promise.

SLUT-BOY: I don't see how this can . . . What's that?

PAPA BEAR: Nothing.

SLUT-BOY: What's the deal? What you doing?

PAPA BEAR: Nothing.

SLUT-BOY: Is that a tie? No way! You're not strangling me! Let me up! Get off!

THE BED SQUEAKS WILDLY

PAPA BEAR (STRAINED): Don't struggle. I weigh twice that of you.

SLUT-BOY: Nnngghh! Nnngghh!

PAPA BEAR: Feels good, doesn't it? I bet you've never felt more alive.

SLUT-BOY: Nnngghh! Nnngghh!

PAPA BEAR: You may come now, if you like. Get it all out. Soak the sheets.

SLUT-BOY: Nnngghh! Nnngghh!

PAPA BEAR (WHISPERING): Hush, my Kings Cross beauty. Hush, hush, hush.

THE SOUND OF THE STRANGULATION CONTINUES FOR AROUND A MINUTE. FURNITURE IS KNOCKED OVER. GLASS SHATTERS. THEN, SILENCE

PAPA BEAR (BREATHLESS AND EXHILARATED): Now, I owe you a promise . . .

SHE HURLS THE RECEIVER TO THE FLOOR, WHERE IT TINKLES INNOCENTLY. BUT SHE can still see it, lurking in the carpet pink and penile, so she leaps from the bed and sprints across the landing and down the stairs to the kitchen, the farthest room in the house. She pours a glass of wine, downs it, pours another. She collapses into a chair. Her face — her whole head no less, and indeed much of the upper part of her body — explodes in tears. How could she be pitched into such misery? What had he done to her with this love of his?

For five minutes she has to regulate her breathing to prevent herself throwing up. The wine pools in her stomach bitterly. In her head many questions behave like maddened insects; she splashes cold water on her face at the kitchen sink and, clutching the food mixer for support, asks her reflection in the darkened window the most important of all: does she still love him?

Yes. Inside she hasn't altered. Her love for him has saddened a little (she can feel this, like a watering of her blood), but it's still a love. It was formed between them, and nothing he's done has caused it to unform. It was like a child, this love, still living when its parents had passed on.

So?

So . . .

If the lad were unconscious and was later allowed to escape, then where was the problem in that? Less than five minutes ago she'd been willing to excuse his bisexuality, willing to think of him laying back enjoying a cigarette, reeking of the boy's arse. Why, then, was a dalliance with the sadistic so utterly inexcusable? Finding both the male and female physique palatable and relishing the sight and sound of pain were practices much misunderstood by the man in the street. Really it was but an alternative approach to life. To most, 2.4 children, a mortgage, a fitted kitchen and a Ford in the drive were important. To others it was their bodies and of what they were capable that mattered. He was obviously less in the first group than she'd thought, more in the second. It was just mistaken identity. He was no Papa Bear.

And perhaps, given time and gentle encouragement, she might one day be ready to join him there, in that place where electric toothbrushes and matching towel sets held no value. Why could the fleshy voyage not be embarked upon together? Put that way it was even romantic. If they shifted the sideboard there would easily be enough space in the living-room to perform a hog-tie; if they cleared the pot plants and push-bikes from the garden shed and painted the inside black and decked it out with padlocks and paddles, it would make an ideal correction room. So long as he took her in his arms afterwards, kissed the weals, told her he loved her.

But then there was the other possibility, that which made her shudder.

What if he were right now enjoying that cigarette, but then stubbing it out on a skinny, cooling chest? What if tomorrow he wasn't speaking at Kitchens 2001 but scouting round for a skip in which to drop a body? Could she still love him, knowing he was this butcher? Could she bear his hand on her waist, his presence in the room, knowing he'd masturbated in a dead boy's mouth?

Yes, she believes momentarily. These days alcoholism and addiction to heroin were recognised disabilities: why not, therefore, the compulsion to kill? Like dependency on a drug it was a societal disorder stemming from an inability to cope with life. And the fitted kitchen industry was ruthless, dog-eat-dog. If anyone had just cause to let off steam now and then it was he. His contribution to society was worth the odd blue corpse. Briefly she wonders if she might even assist; with the baiting, the disposal. Be his second; his Myra. For love, of course.

Or perhaps she could help him walk away; help wean him from the knife. She could plan his schedule so he didn't run into hard up street urchins. She could milk him into the toilet bowl once in the morning and once at bedtime so he wasn't walking round in the day all clogged up and itchy. And if the urge was too wilful she could barricade him in his room, let him scratch the walls and chew the mattress, let him devour the pictures of Boy Bands she would slide under the door. Perhaps she could lull him with medicine, keep him drugged and docile and dreaming of arseholes. Maybe she could go to the root of the problem and carry out a home castration.

She tuts, as if his habit for closing off windpipes were unpleasant but loveable.

But then she is struck by the absurdity of the situation. Who the hell was she trying to fool? Regardless of this love living inside her, she was no murderess. It was ludicrous to pretend she could be cold; ludicrous to think she could give him free reign with a tawse, or to think he doing what he had to someone's son failed to change a thing.

It wasn't the fear of who he was; these things he'd done. It was the fear of being alone waiting while the love they'd made diminished and eventually went away. It was more an ordeal than it dying while they were still together.

HE WHO WAS PAPA BEAR BUT WHO IS NO LONGER CALLS AT EIGHT THE NEXT MORNING, chirpy and cheerful. The phone rings for five minutes before she answers it.

"You sound happy," she says.

"I am."

"Why?"

"I slept well. And because I'm in love."

"Anyone I know?"

"You, silly!"

"Oh."

"Don't you love *me*?" he says.

"Yes, I love you. I can't help but love you."

"What's wrong? You sound depressed."

"Do I?"

"Are you lonely?" he asks. "I am. I'm lonely as hell."

"You are?" she says. "So am I, I guess." Then she says: "But I'll get used to it."

less than perfect

michel faber

Michel Faber was born in Den Haag, Netherlands, in 1960. He spent 1967–1993 in Australia and settled in the Highlands of Scotland in 1993. In 1996, his short story 'Fish' won the Macallan/Scotland On Sunday award. In 1997 another of his stories won the Neil Gunn award, and in 1998 another won the Ian St James award. A collection of his stories, Some Rain Must Fall, was published by Canongate in 1998, and his first novel, Under the Skin, was published by Canongate in 2000, to critical acclaim. It has so far been sold into fifteen languages, and was nominated for the Whitbread Prize.

LACHLAN WAS A DETECTIVE. EIGHTEEN YEARS OLD, ONE O-LEVEL, TWO BIG BONY fists. He'd tried stacking pallets, but it didn't suit his nature. So he was a detective. The pay wasn't great, the hours could be better, but he had no dependants and a sleek new car with automatic windows and a CD player. Criminals watch out: Lachlan's about.

Of course, criminals never suspected Lachlan was about. That was the whole point. They were always amazed when he caught them, as if they would've expected a detective to look like Columbo, with a raincoat and a cigarette. Which just proved how stupid they were. Smoking wasn't allowed, for a start.

The golden rule of being a detective was: Trust No One. Criminals came in all shapes, all ages, all sizes, all sexes. Both sexes, that is.

From a distance, through a dawdling cluster of other bodies, Lachlan saw Mrs Weymouth coming towards him. She was immaculate as always, her dyed auburn hair held in place by spray and metal clips. She hadn't seen him yet; her attention was on a sheaf of papers she held in her hands as she walked. Despite his grudge against her, he had to admire the way she could move so confidently, even on high heels, with her legs constricted in a tight knee-length skirt and a matronly bosom that made her top-heavy. Her ugly square face was uglier for frowning as she read the papers in her hands, yet she moved like a model.

When she was near enough for him not to hit any innocent bystanders, he shot her in the chest with the Magnum. The impact lifted her out of her strapless black shoes, tossing her body through the air like a string bag of fruit. She landed with a smack on the polished floor, chest pumping blood, a burst container. He shot her once more just to make sure, and her flaccid body slid along the floor on its own juice.

"I'd like a word with you, Lachlan," said Mrs Weymouth, drawing abreast with him near the fresh fruit and vegetables.

"Yes?" Lachlan responded, his voice a discreet murmur. All around them in the supermarket aisle, the mass of humanity was shambling by, in weary pursuit of all the good things in life. Reluctantly Lachlan took his eyes off them, knowing that for some, the lure of low cost was not as attractive as no cost at all.

Mrs Weymouth seemed unconcerned by what might be going on behind her back. Instead, she reached down into Lachlan's shopping trolley and fetched out a single banana, one of several he'd only just put in there. She held it up between them and squeezed its yellow shaft with her hard, crimson-nailed fingertips.

"Yes?" he prompted her.

"It's soft," she told him, squeezing the day-glo skin over and over. "See? Soft inside."

"I don't examine them," Lachlan protested mildly. "I just chuck 'em in."

"That's exactly what I mean," said Mrs Weymouth, her voice tight with irritation. "You throw them into the trolley. I've seen you do it. Bananas. Apples. Peaches, even. Then later when you put them back, they're bruised. Next day, they're history."

Lachlan wished she'd talk quieter. It would be just like her, unfair bitch, to blow his cover and then expect him to improve his detection rate.

"Are you saying," he dared to challenge, "that all the fruit here is perfect until I touch it?"

Mrs Weymouth sighed ostentatiously, her eyes half-closing. Her eyelids had about a hundred wrinkles on them: she was as old as his foster-mum — older, even.

"We do our best," she said.

"So do I, Mrs Weymouth," said Lachlan, turning his face away from her, to remind her of the unsupervised multitudes overrunning the store. "I've got to keep my eyes on everybody. Sometimes maybe I'm looking so hard, what's in my hand gets a bit of a bump."

But Mrs Weymouth wasn't finished with him yet.

"I saw a packet of chocolate rollettes you put back on the shelf yesterday," she said, "half-squashed. The damage was caused by the sharp edge of a tin or suchlike while in your trolley. No customer is going to buy those rollettes now. They'll choose a packet that's perfect. The damaged one will end up in the clearance racks, and we'll lose money on it."

Lachlan leaned on the crossbar of his trolley and stared her straight in the eye.

"So sue me," he said. Then, aloud: "Sorry. It won't happen again."

She nodded and turned on her ridiculous heels. He let her go; she wasn't worth the ammo. He had work to do.

ALL DAY, LACHLAN WALKED THE AISLES OF THE SUPERMARKET, TAKING ITEMS OFF the shelves, loading them into his trolley, moving on; then, one by one, he would put the items back, as if he'd changed his mind or discovered he couldn't afford them. All day, as he played this mindless game of selection and deselection, he watched the shoppers, appraising their clothing, scrutinising their hands, reading their faces. In this fluorescent fairyland of unbeatable offers, friendly service and loyalty schemes, hordes of would-be thieves were in constant motion, sniffing for their opportunity. Lachlan couldn't hope to catch them all, but he could catch some.

As soon as he had a suspect, he would follow at a discreet distance. It was easier to spot someone who was thinking of stealing something than someone who'd already done it, so usually when he followed someone, he could expect to catch them in the act. He'd been in this game a long time now, and he knew a thing or two. No one ever stole suddenly, on impulse, innocent up until the moment temptation whispered. They all came into the store intending to steal, it was just a matter of what and when. You could see it on their faces. Guilty as sin, from the word go.

Like any detective, Lachlan found the wiles of his quarry both impressive and pathetic. There really was no limit to what people would try. He'd had a guy with half a watermelon dangling between his legs, in a special sling pinned to his trousers and hidden by a long overcoat. He'd had an old lady with a pair of raw trout in her handbag. He'd had plenty of women hugely pregnant with disposable nappies, rustling as they walked. He'd had a guy with combat trousers, all the pockets bulging so hard with Pilsner cans he could barely walk. He'd had a guy nudging a frozen Christmas turkey along the floor to the cigarette kiosk, then kicking it like a football towards the exit.

Mostly, people would attempt smaller thefts with subtler gestures: a tin of herrings slipped into a coat pocket, a tiny bottle of vanilla essence hidden in a palm, a chocolate bar up the sleeve. There were signs everywhere saying DETECTIVES PATROL THIS STORE but it didn't seem to make any difference.

Maybe no one read those signs, the same way they didn't seem to read anything else in the store — prices, labels, instructions, opening hours, the lot. People never seemed to have a clue where anything was even if they were right underneath a sign telling them. They would stand for ages next to a sign saying BUY TWO GET ONE FREE, and then they'd put two into their trolley anyway. At the checkouts, they'd offer loyalty cards from other supermarkets. Or they'd say, "I'm sorry, I've just realised I don't have any money."

Thickos. Liars. Trust No One.

THERE WAS A GIRL IN HIS SIGHTS NOW, AND SHE WAS GOING TO STEAL SOMETHING for sure. She was only young, with a thick mane of unkempt golden hair and tight jeans. Her grey polyester top was loose though, ideal for concealment. She had big eyes and lips, no make-up. Like him, she had a few pimples here and there.

She was roaming all around the store, pushing her trolley down the middle of the aisles. She wasn't examining the products on the shelves, she was examining the aisles and the people. There was a look people got on their faces when they were searching a supermarket for someone they knew, someone they'd agreed to meet up with. This girl didn't have that look. She didn't care who any of the other shoppers were, he could see that. She was looking for an empty aisle.

Round and round the store she went, like a rat in a maze. He followed her, pushing his trolley almost noiselessly, half-a-dozen steps behind. Sometimes she entered an aisle, sometimes she just glanced into it and passed it by for the next one along. The aisles she didn't bother with were always the ones that had several other shoppers in them.

She came to rest at last in toiletries. Lots of people stole stuff here, mostly the more expensive brands of toothpaste, deodorants, lip salves. Lachlan used lip salve himself, because his top lip was prone to cracking, and his choice of brand was the same one that he'd caught several people stealing. Thieves went for quality. But quality cost them dear, if Lachlan was on the case.

This girl wasn't interested in toiletries, however. She already had what she wanted, in her trolley. It was a long narrow refrigerated dessert, some sort of blueberry or apple Danish packaged in a silver tinfoil tray. She fetched it out, holding it vertically in her fingers. Held like that, side-on to his gaze, it looked like a musical instrument — like one of those recorders he'd been excused from playing at school.

The girl looked right and left, slowly enough for him to melt out of eyeshot at the crucial instant. Then she leaned close to the shelves, as if straining to read the minuscule guarantees printed on some little box. If not completely satisfied, blah blah blah. This does not affect your statutory rights. What were statutory rights? The right to remain silent, the right to one phone call . . . Yes! She was doing it now — a gyration of both elbows and a backward thrust of her pear-shaped buttocks. Lachlan pushed his trolley round the corner, letting it squeak all it liked. The girl turned to face him, her face blank and arrogant with guilt, like a Hollywood movie actress. She'd done a good job with the Danish, he had to admit. It wasn't poking out through the fabric of her top, though her breasts certainly were. He'd seen plenty of people with products falling out of their clothing as they walked, smack onto the floor at their feet. That wouldn't happen to this girl. She'd stowed the Danish inside her jeans, inside the waistband, right next to her flesh probably. Her sex parts were liable to go numb if she didn't make her getaway pronto.

"Excuse me, miss," he said. "Would you mind coming with me for a minute?"

She stiffened, folding her arms across her front. "Why?" she said.

"I think you know why," he said, without emotion.

Leaving her trolley, she walked beside him along the aisle, her face ghastly pale. He took her to the storage bay behind the delicatessen, and into a little windowless room. There was a desk, a chair, a telephone, a filing cabinet, and a fire extinguisher. The bare essentials. Lachlan closed the door.

"OK," he said. "I think we both know what you've got under your top."

Sullenly, the girl reached inside her clothing and pulled out the Danish.

"Have a seat," said Lachlan, indicating the desk, "while I phone the police."

"Please, no," she begged in a small voice.

Lachlan looked her up and down. She had that gun-to-the-head expression, and sweat glistened on her clasped hands.

"There's one thing you can do to make me forget the whole thing," he said. "I think you can guess what that is."

In silence she undressed, pulling her top over her head, exposing her white midriff slightly marked in red by the sharp tinfoil edges of the Danish. Her breasts, barely contained in a faded flesh-coloured bra, were as big as Mrs Weymouth's, a strange sight on such a young body. She left the bra on, but took her jeans and panties off in one motion, hooking her thumbs into the two sets of waistbands. Her pubic hair was golden.

"The bra too," he said.

"Please," she said.

"Do it," he said.

She unhooked her bra, and finally her breasts were revealed, round and perfect like pale pink melons.

"Turn around," he said, "and put your hands against the wall."

He grabbed the cheeks of her bottom and exposed her hairy slit. His erect penis slid in easily, and he ejaculated in about two seconds.

The girl was wheeling her trolley towards the checkouts now; he'd better close in fast or she would get away. It was company policy not to apprehend shoplifters at the checkouts, to save other customers embarrassment.

"Excuse me, miss," he said.

"What for?" she challenged him, sullen like in his vision of her.

"Would you mind accompanying me," he said.

She frowned and bit down hard on her lower lip. She was much better-looking than he'd thought. She had long blonde eyelashes which were only visible at close quarters. Her eyes weren't a regular colour, and they shone with feelings he couldn't identify. Then, suddenly, awkwardly, she smiled, and reached inside her clothing. The stolen Danish was yanked forth, momentarily distending the fabric of her top like that alien baby bursting out of somebody's stomach in that *Alien* movie.

"Here," she said, holding the somewhat buckled package out to him. "Sorry."

Nonplussed, he took hold of it. The tinfoil part was chilly and damp, but the cardboard lid was already warm. Warm from the heat of her flesh.

"Look, I've given it back, OK?" she said, nervously, tossing her hair off her forehead. "Let's just forget all about it. I can't afford it anyway."

Lachlan examined the Danish at a glance. "No one will want to buy this now," he informed her. "Its edges are crumpled. It's as good as wrecked. We'll lose money on it."

Anger and anxiety flashed across the girl's face. "Jesus, what does a crappy frozen dessert mean to you?"

Lachlan tossed it back into her trolley, unmoved. "It's for sale. You didn't pay for it. That's theft. My job is to hand you on to the police. I'm just doing my job."

She stared him straight in the eyes, defiantly at first, then with a slow flush of fear as she glimpsed the impenetrable, steely sureness in him.

"Please," she said then, licking her lips in naked distress. "I've been done for this twice already. Once more, and they'll put me away for sure. I just got hungry for something sweet, that's all. I don't have much money." She gestured limply. "It's hard sometimes."

He drew a deep breath. How to explain to her that life was tough for everyone, everyone in the whole wide dirty world? A bit of slack in one place resulted in a tightening of the screws further down the line. If he let her go, Mrs Weymouth would probably find out about it, and he'd lose his job. Then before you knew it he'd be no better off than this girl was now. He'd lose his car and everything. Conceivably he and this girl would end up standing next to one another at the Job Centre, looking lost and hopeless. There'd be a position going as a store detective and she'd probably get it, because women got everything nowadays, falling into their lap.

"I've got a job to do," was how he summed up these complexities. "Come with me please."

"Wait a minute," she said, her hands trembling as she stepped closer to him. "I . . . I could let you have sex with me."

"What?" said Lachlan. "I beg your pardon?"

Her eyes were shiny, darting back and forth like fish. No one was approaching, though, by almost supernatural luck — all humanity was steering clear of this aisle. And she — so close to him that he could see the pores in her skin and the frightened pulse-beat in her pale throat — she raised her whisper loud above the Muzak, deadly serious: "I could let you fuck me. In the car park. In your car. I know you've got one. I've seen you driving around the town. Your sound system must be about two million watts."

"Look . . ." he said, his voice hoarse all of a sudden.

"I could take all my clothes off," she hissed urgently. "You'd see everything. I'd do whatever you wanted."

He cleared his throat, blushing hot. "I can't just walk out of the store," he grimaced. "It's not allowed."

"Jesus, don't you have tea breaks or something?" she squeaked, almost hysterical, then got hold of herself. "Whenever," she assured him. "Just come out whenever you can, and I'll meet you there."

He gaped at her in disbelief, and she stared back at him imploringly. An old lady trundled round the corner, took one look at them, and passed by, embarrassed. Supermarket life was circling them, waiting for their aisle to be cleared of intimacy and return to normal.

"You must think I'm stupid," said Lachlan.

"No, look," she said in desperation. "Look: I'll give you this . . ." She delved a small pink hand into a pocket of her jeans, and pulled out a key-ring with several keys jingling off it. "It's all my keys," she assured him breathlessly, holding them up by the plastic Tellytubby that linked them. "The keys to everything . . . my front door, my back door, everything . . . this little one's my bike — it's parked just outside, you can see it through the window, there, look!"

With his narrowed eyes he followed where she was pointing, and, sure enough, there was a bicycle blurrily visible through the wall of plate glass, just under the giant affiched letters saying ꜱᗡƎƎИ ꓤUOY ᒐᒐA ꓤOᖷ.

"I can't do without these keys, do you understand?" she pleaded. "I can't even get home. I have to have them." She pressed the keys against his dangling hand, and let them go. Instinctively he grabbed them rather than let them fall to the ground; it was a reflex action. She put both her soft palms on his right shoulder and lifted herself up on tiptoes to murmur in his ear. "You've got me right where you want me. I'll be waiting." And she ran off, leaving her trolley behind.

Lachlan steadied himself for a few moments, aware that inside his clothes he was soaked with perspiration. He wiped his forehead and mouth, inspected his sleeve. The news was not good. God knows what the customers would think, seeing him in this state. The first thing to do was get rid of the Danish — if Mrs Weymouth saw it she would go ballistic. Furtively, heart pounding, he rushed the damp and damaged specimen to the frozen goods section, fearing the old woman's eyes on him with every step. He hid the Danish under others of its kind, piling the straight and perfect ones over it two layers deep. This done, undetected, he relaxed a little. The light in the supermarket seemed less harsh, the central heating less absurdly high. Mrs Weymouth was at the far end of the store, pretending to care about a disabled shopper. The clock above the community noticeboard said four thirty-eight. Another three-and-a-half hours and he was a free man. For the next little while he walked the girl's trolley around the supermarket, putting items back on the shelves. Spaghetti. Bread. Peanut butter. Sugar Puffs. Milk. Sanitary pads. He wasn't sure if he could cope with a vagina that was bleeding. It wasn't clean, somehow.

AT EIGHT PM, AS THE LAST SHOPPERS WERE BEING USHERED OUT OF THE SUPER-market into the summer dusk, Lachlan was already outside, standing right next to the girl's bicycle, waiting. Not born yesterday, he had a sick feeling she wouldn't show up, but still he hoped she might. He ran his sharp eyes back and forth across all the cars parked in neat rows, in case she was hiding amongst them. He remembered her very well, physically. A single glimpse of her face or her behind would have been enough to identify her, if she'd been anywhere about. Golden rule: Trust No One. As more and more cars pulled away, there were fewer places where a girl could be hiding.

Lachlan consulted the watch on his bony wrist. Eight minutes had passed in what had felt like twenty seconds. Nothing sexual was going to happen now. He tried to imagine some way he could get revenge. God, how she must despise him, if she was willing to lose her bike just to avoid a few seconds of unwanted attention. Maybe she was scared of him. That would be a tragedy, if that was all it was. It could have been a fantastic experience. She would have got her keys back; he would have found out what intercourse was like. She might even have enjoyed it. There was nothing wrong with his sex organs, that was for sure.

What was he going to do with her bike? He could take it away with him, sell it maybe. As long as he didn't get in trouble with the police. Like all private detectives, he had an uneasy relationship with the boys in blue. One of them had stopped him once, on one of those long sleepless nights when he'd taken the car out for a drive, CDs belting out into the lonely dark. The cop had told him it was a mystery how a moron like Lachlan had ever been judged fit for a car license. That was the sort of crack you didn't forget in a hurry.

Lachlan looked at the girl's bicycle again. His car, he suddenly remembered, didn't have a roof rack. Never mind the bike, then: he could maybe use the chain and the padlock for something. Keep something of his own safe, something he hadn't thought of yet. And her bike would most likely get stolen during the night, which would serve her right. He slipped the smallest of the keys into the bike's padlock, and twisted. Through his fingers he could sense something wasn't right. Nothing clicked or fell open.

"Hey!" a male voice shouted from not far away. "Hey!"

Lachlan tried to pull the key out, but it was gripped tight in the lock. An athletic-looking man with grey hair and paint-spattered training clothes had set two evenly-weighted shopping bags down on the asphalt and began to stride towards Lachlan from the vaulted entrance of the supermarket.

Panicking, Lachlan let the keys go and ran to his own car. It was instantly identifiable by the silver demister strips on the back window, the little Celtic flag on the aerial, and the big warning stickers about what would happen if anyone tried to break in and steal the potent black metallic speakers within. A new addition to the vehicle's distinguishing features, however, was one that Lachlan noticed only as he was struggling to unlock the door. All along the driver's side, gouged deeply into the paintwork with some sort of sharp instrument, was the word WANKER.

Finally bursting in, he slammed himself into safety and started the motor. With scarcely a second's pause he began to reverse the car, dizzily relieved to find that the bicycle's owner had given up the pursuit and was returning to his shopping bags. Not worth it. Lachlan pulled on the brake and sat tight, loath to be pushed now that the heat was off. The bicycle man cycled away; Lachlan memorised his distinguishing features for future reference. After a few more minutes the car park lights, synchronised with the sunset somehow, glowed all around him. Mrs Weymouth and the big boss were locking the supermarket's entrance inside a big trellis of iron bars. The big boss pointed a device at a hidden alarm and pressed the trigger. Then he and Mrs Weymouth walked to the same car. When they had driven off, Lachlan reversed fully into the empty expanse of tarmac. The keys to everything lay discarded near the bike stands, for the girl to retrieve if she was still out there somewhere, spying on the scene, waiting for him to make his move. Blinking away tears, Lachlan edged his precious injured vehicle towards the exit, conscious that if he allowed his anger and his hurt to get on top of him, he might crash the car in the dangerous traffic beyond the supermarket, and lose more than he had lost already. In the rear-view mirror, his own face was reflected back at him undisguised, the hare-lip vivid and glistening above his malformed teeth. Looking right and left, forwards and backwards, he indicated to the world where he was meaning to go. Then, gunning the engine, he followed through and left them all for dead.

family game

andrew humphrey

Andrew Humphrey is married with two sons and living in Norwich. He spends most of his daylight hours in a city centre office where the work is numbing but the people excellent. Andrew has supported Norwich City FC for thirty years which he thinks probably explains a lot.

ABOVE THE MEADOW TO MY LEFT A KESTREL OR A SPARROWHAWK HOVERS BRIEFLY in the cloudless sky then drops into the long grass as though weighted with lead shot.

I frown, my face pressed against the window. Julie's driving. It's hot outside. The windows in our Sierra Estate are closed and the air-conditioning gushes frigid air across my face and legs. The noise of it makes conversation difficult. Which suits us both.

The meadow has gone now. I wonder if it was a Kestrel or a Sparrowhawk. I can't remember which is bigger. I don't suppose that it matters much to the small wrecked thing at the bottom of its dive.

We take a left turn at the next crossroads and then the next right down a dirt track. The track is rutted and hard as iron. The car shudders and Julie swears and grips the steering wheel harder.

"Nearly there," I say.

Julie grunts.

It is late September but the month long heatwave shows no sign of ending. The fields that trundle close by look drained and tired.

"I said I'd drive," I say.

"I'm fine driving. It's nothing to do with driving. It's this bloody heat."

"Well, it's not hot in here," I say, raising my voice above the roar of the air-conditioning.

"Speak for yourself. You're not six months pregnant, are you?"

There's not much I can say to that so as usual I take refuge in silence.

MY SISTER'S HOUSE IS SET IN A DOZEN ACRES OF NORFOLK WILDERNESS THAT IS itself engulfed by miles of fens and heaths and brief dense woods.

We approach from the east. The driveway is long and narrow and winds beneath the branches of beech trees. Brittle sunlight angles through the leaves.

Julie wears a blue cotton maternity dress. Her face is red. Her eyes and mouth are tight with concentration. Her fair hair is pulled back into a pigtail, held in place by a black velvet scrunchy.

"I'm having a drink," Julie says as we pass a vast mottled lawn and approach the shingled parking area at the front of the house. "Some wine with dinner."

"I didn't say anything."

"You don't have to. I know you disapprove."

I close my eyes and say nothing.

"I don't suppose a couple of glasses of wine will hurt your precious baby."

"*Our* baby," I say slowly, eyes still closed.

She drives past a fountain in the middle of the shingled area and parks next to an ivy-covered retaining wall.

"Can't smoke, can't drink."

"Julie, you've never smoked."

"And as for sex, well . . . all I can say is it's a wonder the poor little sod ever got conceived in the first place."

"For Christ's sake, don't start that again. It's Karen's birthday. Let's try to be nice, can we? Just for the weekend?"

"Oh, I'm sorry, Paul. I forgot. Mustn't upset your sister. God forbid."

I sigh deeply and push the car door open. The heat is ludicrous. The contrast from the car's frigid interior makes me giddy.

It takes Julie almost a minute to extract herself fully from the driver's seat.

"Thanks for your help," she says. She runs a hand across her forehead, squinting up at the near-white sky. "Fucking hell, it's like an oven out here."

JULIE HATES MY SISTER'S HOUSE. I LOVE IT. IT'S OVER FIVE HUNDRED YEARS OLD although most of the original building is lost amid extensions, additions, reconstructions. A melody of styles and fads and fashions coexist here. Three floors, four en-suite bedrooms, a vast staircase that zigzags up from the entrance hall to wide landings on each floor. At one point a turret was added to the eastern edge of the house for no apparent reason. Gargoyles adorn the guttering along the western face. Marble columns sit either side of the oak front door. Stone steps lead down from the door to the drive.

Karen meets us at the bottom step. She's fifty today. A young fifty. I'm nearly twenty years younger. She's tall and willowy. She wears a short white cotton dress. Her legs are slim and brown. She has an elegance inherited from our mother. I don't. Her hair is dark and cut fashionably short. She looks younger when she smiles and she smiles frequently. She's smiling now, slender arms outstretched. "Julie, you look wonderful."

"Well, I feel like shit."

"Darling, you're simply glowing. Pregnancy suits you."

I wince. Julie's eyebrows arch. Her face is the colour of boiled ham and sweat cuts dark streaks through her fair hair. "Really?" she says.

"Oh yes. I expect it's a bit wretched in this heat, but I'm sure the worst is over. It's all downhill from here, you'll see."

The women embrace briefly. "That's such a comfort. Remind me, Karen. How many children have you had exactly?"

Karen's smile falters, but only a fraction and only for a moment.

"You get in the shade, love," she says, ushering Julie into the hallway. "Go through to the kitchen. Philip's fixing drinks. He's so looking forward to seeing you."

I bet he is, I think.

Julie waddles into the gloom. Karen gives me a look. "Poor Paul," she says.

She rests her hands on my shoulders and kisses my cheek. Her lips are cool. I smell her perfume. I put a hand on her slim waist.

"Poor Paul indeed," I say. I feel the tightness in my stomach ease.

"You know it's only her hormones, don't you?" she says.

"I'm not so sure," I say. "I think aliens have abducted the real Julie and sent this thing in her place."

She pulls away from me and I let her go reluctantly. She reaches a hand to my face. Her fingers are cool. "You need a shave," she says.

"I thought I'd try a beard."

Her nose wrinkles. "Oh don't. It won't suit you. You look younger clean shaven. More handsome."

I nod and look down. She wears white sandals with modest heels. Her toenails are painted burgundy.

Karen sighs. "Poor Julie," she says. "She was such a sweet young thing." She pauses. "It's not just the pregnancy, is it?"

I look up at her then my eyes cut away to the heat haze in the distance. "No. It's not just the pregnancy."

I follow Karen through the hallway. The carpet is crimson and black and feels inches thick. The woodwork in the hallway and the staircase are deep mahogany. There's an unlit open fireplace opposite surrounded with glazed terra-cotta tiles.

Philip and Julie are in the kitchen, chatting easily. Naturally an aga dominates one wall. The kitchen is larger than our lounge. There's a breakfast bar in the corner and a pine table that could seat a dozen at a pinch monopolises the far end.

I shake hands with Philip. Reluctantly. His grip is firm and damp and repulsive all at the same time.

"Just chatting up your little lady," he says, "hope you don't mind." He pats Julie's stomach. "Who's a clever girl?" he says.

Julie giggles. The last time I patted her stomach she told me to fuck off. I stare at her and she avoids my gaze.

Philip is tall and broad with a bright ruddy face and sandy hair. His complexion owes much to his malt whisky addiction. He's a Londoner. I try not to hold it against him. He made a small fortune in scrap metal in the seventies and a larger one from recycled building materials a decade later. I could just about forgive his borderline fascism and his obsession with all things Thatcher if he wasn't such an unreconstructed, loudmouthed twat.

But he is. And my sister married him. Shit happens, as they say.

Philip drinks some whisky and clinks his glass against Julie's glass, which is full of ice and a clear liquid.

"I hope that's lemonade," I say. I know how boorish I sound but I can't help myself.

"Of course it's lemonade," Philip booms, aiming a hammy wink at Julie. She winks back and giggles again. She looks at me briefly. "Lemonade," she says, then looks back at Philip.

"A bit early isn't it?" I say.

Philip rolls his eyes. "It's gone four, Paul. Anyway, it's Karen's birthday. We're celebrating, aren't we, Julie?"

She giggles yet again. In agreement. I resist the urge to throttle her. Instead I close my eyes and wish I were somewhere else. Beirut, perhaps.

Then Karen's there, her hand on my arm. "Come on, Paul. Have a beer. I'll get a cold one from the fridge."

I smile my thanks. "And happy birthday," I say. "Your present's in the car. I'll get it later."

"No rush, no rush," she says. She smiles and drinks. Her lips are wet with wine and there's a look of quiet desperation in her eyes.

"Flirt a little more, why don't you?" It's just after five-thirty and Julie and I are unpacking in our room.

"Well, at least he notices me."

"Believe me, with Philip, that's not a compliment."

"He's always liked me. At least he's got some life in him."

I slip my boxer shorts and clean socks into a drawer in a small oak dresser. It smells faintly of lavender.

"It's nice being fancied again. I've forgotten what it's like. When did you last touch me, Paul? My memory's not that good."

I keep my back to her. "I'm scared of hurting the baby. You know that."

"And what was your excuse before the baby, Paul?"

"I got you pregnant, didn't I? Must have done something right."

"That's a matter of opinion."

I turn and look at her. Her mouth is set in a thin hard line that I've come to recognise and loathe. I wonder where the real Julie is. I'm sure she's in there somewhere. I hope she is.

She turns and folds her navy maternity knickers neatly and puts them away. "Anyway, I can't compete with the lovely Karen, can I?"

I stop what I'm doing. "What's that supposed to mean?"

"The way you look at her."

"She's my sister."

"Precisely."

"What does that mean?"

"You work it out."

I turn back to the dresser. I open a drawer, close it again. "You've gone too far this time," I say.

"If you blame it on my hormones I'll hit you, I swear I will," Julie says.

For a moment I think of hitting *her*. I consider it in some detail. Then a voice floats up from the landing below. Philip. Who else. "Must be for you," I say. My voice seems flat and stiff.

Julie's face changes. She opens the door and shouts down. "Coming, Philip."

Downstairs I say, "Shooting rabbits? You don't like guns. You don't like rabbits. This makes no sense."

Julie stands with her arms folded and stares past my left shoulder. Philip breezes into the hallway. Despite the heat he wears a Barbour jacket. He carries a broken twelve bore over one arm.

"Just bagging some bunnies, Paul. You're welcome to join us." He sees the look on my face. "Got to be done, mate. Little bastards'll overrun us otherwise."

"But Julie hates guns. Hates shooting things."

Philip shrugs. "Well now she wants to give it a try. No big deal. Perhaps it's her hormones."

Julie giggles.

"Let them go," Karen says. She sits on the stairs behind us. Her legs are crossed. Her chin rests in one hand. She has a glass of pale wine in the other.

Philip turns. "Sure you don't want to come, love?" There's a sneer in his voice that I don't like at all.

"You go on," she says, not looking at him. "Just keep the poor little things away from me."

There's an interior door, a small porch, then the large oak front door. Philip and Julie go through them into the early evening heat. Some of it seeps into the shaded hall. Philip's voice and Julie's giggles recede.

We sigh simultaneously.

I sit next to Karen on the stairs. "How the hell did you end up with him?" I've asked the question before and she gives the usual answer.

"He was quite a catch back in '75. Big hair, big lapels. Bundles of one pound notes in his back pocket. Enough to turn a girl's head."

"Sounds a lot easier in those days. I think I was born too late."

We look at each other briefly and say nothing. The silence is comfortable.

Then Karen says, "I like it when Philip goes shooting." She pauses and I look at her. As if on cue both barrels of the shotgun echo in the distance. "There's always a chance he'll blow his fucking head off."

Her face shows no expression. But I catch the sparkle in her green eyes and start to laugh. We hear the gun again, bruising the quiet of the Norfolk afternoon.

BEFORE DINNER I SHAVE CAREFULLY AND PUT ON SOME AFTERSHAVE AND A CLEAN shirt. Sweat gathers immediately on my back and beneath my arms. Julie wears make-up for the first time in months.

A beautifully set rectangular oak table dominates the dining room. We eat by candlelight. Karen serves venison and roast vegetables. Philip drinks whisky with his meal. Karen and I drink white wine; Julie keeps her glass topped up from a bottle of Californian red.

I eat slowly and watch Julie drink. Eventually I smile and say softly, "Don't you think you've had enough, love?"

She looks at me and shakes her head. Her made-up face shines in the candlelight. I realise she repulses me.

"Let her be," Philip says, smiling. "Got to enjoy yourself sometime, haven't you Julie? Let your hair down."

She looks at Philip. "That's right," she says. She simpers a little, but at least she doesn't giggle.

I feel I can't leave it alone. "But the baby . . ."

"Oh, fuck the baby," Julie says, turning to me, her face changing again. Too much mascara, I think. And the lipstick's all wrong. "I should have tried gin and a coat hanger months ago."

There's a small, charged silence. Even Philip looks embarrassed. Then Karen says, "More vegetables, Paul?"

I take some parsnips and honey glazed carrots. Her green eyes meet mine. Her make-up is minimal, I notice. A touch of lip gloss, a little blusher. Her nails are painted the colour of dark wine. She wears an ivory silk blouse and a long black skirt.

Somehow we make it to dessert. Then Philip asks me about work and my heart sinks. "It's fine thanks," I say.

"The cut and thrust of local government. Heady stuff."

I smile stiffly.

"Pity about that promotion. Julie told me you didn't get it."

"Perhaps next year."

"Perhaps."

He leaves a small silence and like a fool I fill it. "I know it doesn't sound much. Working for the council. But it does matter. Local democracy and all that. Working for the people."

"Absolutely," Philip says. "Vital stuff. I'm sure you're a crucial, if rather small cog in a well-oiled machine. God knows what we'd do without you."

Sweat beads his forehead. It's probably seventy-percent proof. Julie watches, fascinated, a spoonful of toffee roulade halfway to her lips. Karen seems somewhere else entirely. I can't say I blame her.

Philip is now primed for his obligatory self made man speech and he doesn't disappoint. I tune him out. I drink some wine and wait for him to come up for air.

LATER, STILL AT THE TABLE, WE DRINK COFFEE AND BRANDY. PHILIP SMOKES A CIGAR. "Could've had a proper party," he says, waving his arms expansively. He is, I realise, extremely pissed. "No expense spared, that's what I said. Could've had my mates round. They'd have livened the place up. But no. The birthday girl wants family, the birthday girl gets family." He smiles unpleasantly.

"The only family I have left," Karen says softly, gazing into her coffee.

"Apart from me," Philip says.

Karen ignores him. She fingers her necklace. "Thanks for this, you two. It's beautiful. Did you choose it, Julie?"

Julie sips her brandy. "No. I left it to Paul. Same as I leave most things to Paul. Like responsibility for contraception, for instance."

"More coffee," Karen says quickly, but it's too late.

"What's this?" Philip says. "Bit of a slip up, was it Paul? Careless, old boy. Very careless. Slipshod. Pretty much what I'd expect from the council, come to think of it."

I feel my face redden. "I really don't think . . . "

"Oh, forget it, old boy. No need to apologise. Anyway, it suits you, Julie, it really does. You look wonderful. Wonderful. I've always had a thing about pregnant women." He turns to Karen. "Haven't I, love?"

Karen stares at the table. She puts her hands to her mouth. Then she stands, puts the coffee things methodically onto the tray and leaves the room.

Fifteen years ago she had two miscarriages in eighteen months.

Philip shrugs and smiles at Julie. I imagine sliding the barrels of his shotgun into his mouth and pulling both triggers.

LATER THAT NIGHT I LAY ON MY BACK IN BED WITH MY HANDS LINKED BEHIND MY head and listen to Julie's snores. She lays on her side with her back to me. There's about six inches between us.

I gaze up at the ceiling. The curtains and window are open. Moonlight angles in. The air is stale and hot. As though it's been recycled too often. The wilderness surrounding my sister's house is utterly quiet.

The volume of Julie's snoring increases and the tone deepens.

Ten years ago, in late November, we rented a cottage close to Derwent Water. It pissed down all weekend. We made love almost continuously. We touched and talked and laughed. The details have gone; the clothes she wore, what we talked about. But I remember her smile and how her eyes shone. I remember my mild astonishment that I could be the reason for another person's happiness.

It's been downhill ever since. Perhaps it always is. With almost geological slowness we've inched apart, minute by minute, hour by hour, until, years later, there's a fucking great chasm between us that neither of us has the first idea how to bridge. Or if we even want to.

And then there's the baby. I'm sure it's a boy. May as well call the poor little sod Damien and tattoo 666 on his arse.

These things happen. Nobody's fault. Careless, though. Bloody careless. I close my eyes. Sleep still seems an age away.

I WAKE SUDDENLY. I'M LYING ON MY STOMACH, MY FACE BURIED IN THE PILLOW. The pillow is wet. I roll onto my back. I grab the alarm clock and hold it close to my face. Just after three. Something's missing. No snores. I fling out an arm. Julie's side of the bed is empty. I'm surprised that I care. She's probably in the bathroom so I wait a while and wonder what woke me.

Ten minutes later I pad down the three flights of stairs. The carpet is soft beneath my bare feet. I wear only a pair of blue cotton pyjama trousers. The stairs creak faintly under my weight.

In the hallway I hear a sound from the kitchen. Someone giggling. When I push the door open the brightness of the light dazzles me. Julie and Philip are standing by the breakfast bar. They move apart from one another almost comically. Philip has on a white T-shirt and grey flannel shorts. Julie wears just her pink maternity nightdress. It occurs to me suddenly how large her breasts have become.

"Couldn't sleep," Philip says. "Fancied a drink." He holds up the tumbler in his right hand. "Want one?"

"No," I say.

"Thought I heard a noise," Julie says. "Thought I'd better have a look. Didn't know it was Philip, did I?" She sees me looking at the empty glass on the breakfast bar, inches from her hand. "Needed something to calm my nerves," she says.

"Purely medicinal," I say.

"That's right."

I cock my head to one side. "What's the problem? Why do you both look so guilty?"

"We don't," Philip says.

"Yes you do. You're both blushing like hell." At least I think they are. It's hard to tell with their complexions. "What's up, Philip? Don't tell me you were going to pin her over the kitchen table."

Julie gasps. Philip says, "Don't be so crude, man. You've got it all wrong."

"Whatever," I say. "I'm going to bed. Goodnight." I close the door behind me. I feel a strange elation as I climb the stairs. A bit like a sugar high. I know I'll pay for it later.

I'm still awake when Julie comes to bed. She lies on her side, her back to me, without speaking. I turn towards her. I realise with some surprise that I have an erection. The tip of it brushes Julie's nightdress. I move a fraction closer.

"What are you doing," Julie says.

I say nothing, just move closer still, so that I'm pressed up against her buttocks. She wriggles away and I follow her. "I thought you wanted it," I say. I try to push the head of my cock between her thighs.

"Don't flatter yourself," she says. She pushes me back and sits on the edge of the bed. "If you're that desperate go and have a wank."

I roll out of bed. Clumsily. My forlorn erection gets snagged in the sheets. My face is hot. I can think of nothing to say so I follow my cock out of the bedroom door.

DOWNSTAIRS AGAIN I GO TO THE KITCHEN. IT'S DARK AND EMPTY. I DRINK SOME water. My face and chest are wet with sweat. In one of the living rooms I open the French doors and step onto a small paved area that leads to an expanse of lawn. The concrete is cold beneath my feet. In the moonlight I can see as far as the first huddle of trees. Beyond that shadows lurk. The air is thick and still and difficult to breathe.

I smell Karen before I hear her. Perfume and shampoo. I turn and she pauses a couple of feet from me. She should look older with her make-up gone but she doesn't. Her face is pale. She wears a knee-length black silk nightdress. Her arms and bare shoulders are brown but her skin turns white as it dips towards her breasts.

"Paul?" she says. Tentatively.

I don't trust myself to speak. My throat feels thick, my eyes hot.

I put my hands to my face. "Oh, shit," I say.

I hear the rustle of her nightdress as she moves towards me. She takes me in her arms. My hands drop to her waist and I pull her closer. Her hands stroke the back of my neck. My face is by her throat. I can feel her pulse there, close to my lips. I smell her perfume and her clean hair.

I feel my erection again, pressing hard against her flat stomach. For a moment neither of us moves. Then she withdraws a fraction and so do I. I pull my face from her neck.

"God, I'm sorry," I say.

She smiles at me but her cheeks are red. "Don't be silly," she says.

I realise there are tears on my face and on hers too.

Her hands are on my shoulders now. She's close enough that I can feel her breath. My erection still strains towards her. Neither of us looks down.

It feels as though my nerves are on the outside of my skin. Her fingertips move a fraction and my senses scream. My heart hammers in my chest. I need to come. The merest touch will do it. God forgive me but I want her fingers to drop to my chest and then lower still.

My hands are on her hips and her skin is hot beneath the silk. I try, minutely, to pull her towards me, to give her the slightest excuse to hold me again. But she resists. I look into her eyes and what I see there breaks my heart. She takes her hands from my shoulders and my arms drop to my sides. She leans forward from a safe distance and kisses my cheek. It's a chaste kiss. A sister's kiss. But it burns anyway.

Then she's gone.

I stand for a while in the darkness and let the decades of shame and guilt and self-disgust have their way with me.

A LITTLE LATER I SIT IN THE KITCHEN, SMOKING. I GAVE UP FOUR YEARS AGO BUT what the hell. I hear a noise outside the kitchen door. I hope that it's Karen. Or

Julie at a pinch. But my luck holds and it's Philip. "You again," he says.

"Apparently."

He fetches his tumbler from the draining board and half fills it with whisky. He looks at me. "Have you been nicking my fags?"

"Didn't think you'd mind. Considering you tried to shag my wife."

"Don't start that again."

"Don't get me wrong. You can fuck her until her teeth rattle for all I care."

He swallows some whisky, then takes a cigarette from the packet of Silk Cut and lights it. "It's Karen you should be worried about."

"Why?"

"She's lying upstairs crying her eyes out. Have you upset her?"

"Don't be a prat. It's probably you."

He opens the kitchen door and flicks ash into the darkness. "I can't hurt her anymore, Paul. You know that."

"You still have a fucking good try, don't you?"

"It's you, Paul. Not me. She's always been more than a sister to you, hasn't she?"

I look up at him sharply. "What's that supposed to mean?"

"Easy tiger," he says. "How old were you when your mum died? Five? Six? And your dad was long gone. She brought you up, didn't she? Made sacrifices for you. The state you and Julie are in, it breaks her heart."

He drains his glass and puts it back in the sink. He goes back to the doorway and blows smoke into the night.

"You broke her heart, you bastard," I say, "and her spirit."

He still has his back to me. He laughs. "I still love her, really. It's just a game we play. You'll understand when you grow up."

I stand quietly. On the floor, next to the aga, there's a black wrought iron doorstop in the shape of a Golden Retriever. I pick it up. It's heavy. Philip finishes his cigarette and flicks it into the night. I watch its tip cartwheel through the darkness. I move up to him and bring the doorstop down onto the back of his head. He grunts and falls forward. He stays on his knees for a moment, wavering. His breathing is rapid, irregular. I hit him again. He crumples forward.

His scalp is awash with blood, dark in the moonlight, flooding his fair hair. I'm not sure if he's breathing.

I put the doorstop on the concrete outside. I step backwards into the kitchen, close the door, lock it.

I stand in silence, straining for signs of movement from upstairs. Absurdly, I half expect to hear sirens in the distance and then the hiss of displaced gravel as the police cars pull up in the drive.

I sit at the kitchen table for half an hour, drinking Philip's whisky. The house is still quiet. I pad into the hallway and take our car keys from the telephone table. I go out through the front door, lock it from the outside, push the keys through the letterbox.

The Sierra's pedals feel strange under my bare feet. I start the engine. The seat belt is cold against my chest. As the headlights sweep across the meadow rabbits scatter for the long grass.

It's four-thirty in the morning and owls are hunting beneath a gibbous moon.

adele and harvey

tim casson

Tim Casson was born in Birmingham and now lives in Cardiff. He's worked in the theatre for some time and has met a few A-list celebrities like Anthony Hopkins, Vanessa Redgrave, Richard Harris and lots of TV 'stars'. He has lots of amusing anecdotes that would be too dodgy to print and are best left in the pub. Tim's been renovating his house for the past few years and working full-time, so hasn't had much time to write – this is his first published story.

PEOPLE DOWN THE LOCAL PUB ARE GETTING CURIOUS. THEY'VE READ HER REVIEWS in the newspapers. They want to know how such a thing is possible. I suppose it's only natural, this curiosity. I mean, how does a talentless, overweight chancer like myself manage to score such an incredible girlfriend? Okay, so they don't come right out and say that, but I'm sure it's what they're thinking.

And the black tie and evening gown bunch. Rich cliquey bastards who interrogate me at first-night parties and after-show functions. A kind of sport. A kind of social ritual to go with the champagne and canapés. Subtle layers of snobbery and innuendo.

A typical query: So, tell me Harvey, how did you two . . . you know . . . ?
Meet?
Polite nods and smiles all round.
There's this friend, I explain for the hundredth time, works for a box-making manufacturer. Yes, *boxes*. You know the things, not glamorous, just boring old containers. Anyway, my business had just gone under so this friend pulls a few strings and fixes me a job in sales. They — the box makers — attend the occasional corporate function. That's how I managed to get an invite to the ballet and afterwards the sponsor's party where I met her. My new employers sponsor her company, supply heavy-duty flight cases for touring equipment and get a mention in the programme. Simple as that.

Not convinced, these rich cliquey bastards probe for a secret — there has to be a *secret*! They scrutinise me freely, regardless of my own sensitivities. All they see is an ordinary-looking Joe in his late twenties. Not particularly attractive and a lottery win from parity with *their* bank balances. Fringe getting a bit thin, soft midriff, chunky legs. Too many beers and late-night curries. There's got to be *something*, they think. My telephone voice, persuasive enough to have acquired fifteen new clients in the last month, attracts suspicion. He must be a sinister, manipulative brainwasher, they figure. Maybe he runs his own cult.

Surely a case of opposites attract, someone says. You're not in the arts. What does she . . . ?
See in me?
I shrug. I grin. There's the answer. Some smiles are phoney and betray a fawning personality. Mine is natural, and it catches. Never practised it or anything. There she was, in the theatre function room, staring blankly at the ornate gold-leaf plaster moulding above my head. Harassed by fawning personalities not unlike yourselves. I smiled, she smiled. The beginning of something.

SOMETIMES LATELY I'VE BEEN WAKING VERY EARLY, BEFORE FIRST LIGHT. ANTICIpating like a child who suspects something exciting is going to happen that day. Sunrise lights her curtains a rich deep gold, gradually brings her bedroom — with all its feminine touches — to life. The changing light adds form to the dark shape curled under the cotton sheet beside me.

Unfortunately she dances in her sleep. I'm wary of her reflexes, a heel to the groin, an elbow in the eye. So much latent energy — it's scary. Taut, soft, tight-muscled. When I brush against her I wonder whether I'm in the lair of some sleeping serpent goddess, a deadly shape-shifter. I adjust the sheet slightly, half expecting a yellow predator's eye, yet see only the beautiful Adele. I move closer, pressing my erection against her smooth buttocks. She stirs, languid, purrs sleepily.

Adele emits a powerful sexual aura. Without realising, she stirs men up, and women also. She walks into a room and conversations wind down to a murmur. The mood alters, slows, quickens, rights itself to her pace. And yet, occasionally, those large brown eyes show undisguised fear. She seems to be searching for someone she can trust, to share a secret with perhaps. At such times all I see is a young girl abandoned in a dark forest.

Whenever we go out, the leering stares of men are a constant reminder of Adele's beauty. Not that I need reminding. It does make me self-conscious about my physique though. Adele smiles and says she likes me the way I am. She must be the only one that feels that way. I get the idea her friends disapprove of our relationship, and Madame Julie, her seventy-five-year-old choreographer, is openly hostile.

Madame Julie doesn't think I'm good enough for you, I say, examining myself critically in Adele's dressing room mirror. The golf ball light bulbs framing the mirror make my image even more unappealing — a comical parody of the handsome male dancer that should really be occupying this space.

I think I'm in the wrong room, or is it the wrong body? I murmur, gripping a squidge of chest-fat. Sometimes I feel like an upstart.

Adele shrugs. You're not making any sense, she says.

She likes melon after class, four varieties, peeled, seeded, cubed in a bowl, ice-cold.

Madame made a snap judgement that night, I say, at the Opera House. Maybe I don't drive the right car, not rich enough, too fat and ugly or something.

Adele slips another pink cube between her lips. You're getting paranoid, she says, slurping juice, sucking fingertips.

It's impossible not to kiss her. She giggles. Her mouth is sticky, her tongue cool, sweet-tasting. She's wearing just a grey Lycra-skin top and shorts, damp and warm from her exertions. The Lycra clings to her body, revealing every detail.

I like you the way you are, she says, unzipping me and slipping her hand inside my pants. She laughs as I gasp at her cold fingertips.

I FIRST MEET THE CHAIN-SMOKING MADAME JULIE AT A PARTY — THE LAST NIGHT of *Giselle*. A fragile old woman with a cane. Instead of shaking my hand she tilts her head disapprovingly, prods my soft belly with a shrivel-skinned, arthritic finger.

Who did you say you were with? she asks, voice croaking with the sticky deposits of countless unfiltered cigarettes. A quick glance to check she has everyone's attention, then, What! *My* Adele, surely not?

Ignore the frosty old bitch, Dean advises me. Dean is head of touring wardrobe and my only friend.

She thinks all the girl dancers belong to her, Dean continues. Like she's given birth to them or something. They're her 'angels', her babies, her pets. She's a tyrant, and quite obviously insane.

Dean is one of the few gay men I've met who are entirely at ease with themselves and their surroundings. Nothing to prove. No statements, exaggerated public displays, no contrived camp, just a naturally amiable personality. He's the only person who really speaks to me. Everyone else, with the exception of Madame Julie, is polite yet distant. I have my uses. Dean's passion is for company gossip.

Being an outsider makes me the ideal audience.

Madame *was* pronounced dead but unfortunately someone resuscitated her, Dean says between slurps of red wine.

Dead?

As dead as a stuffed bird. Okay, I exaggerate . . . a little. She was supposed to be retired but for some reason they wheeled her back in to direct *Nutcracker*. Perhaps I should sell her the idea of retiring early from planet Earth — or euthanasia as it's more commonly known.

I laugh. She does seem very old and frail, I say.

She was an exceptional dancer in her day, he says, very beautiful. Hard to imagine that brittle body once pounded the boards. Time is *such* a bastard.

I think she hates me, I say.

Dean grins and says, Don't worry, you're not alone. She hates all Adele's boyfriends.

All? How many are there? I wonder.

SOMETIMES WHEN SHE DANCES, ESPECIALLY DURING A MORE DIFFICULT MOMENT in a ballet, I've noticed the beginnings of a small smile appear in one corner of her mouth. Nobody else has said anything about this. As far as I know it hasn't been caught on camera yet. Makes me want to wander over, pick her up in my arms, squeeze her, spin her around a couple of times for good measure. I don't mention this to anyone because they wouldn't allow me to watch from the wings if they thought a dumpy guy might bolt on stage at a critical moment in the performance. They don't like me watching from the wings anyway. The audience would be horrified, I'm sure.

Just now everyone backstage is too engrossed in the performance to notice me. Two pretty young women, not long out of college and looking chic in black, watch Adele's every move. A technician who resembles a middle-aged biker is similarly transfixed.

I stand behind a very tall flat screen designed to mask backstage activity from the audience. There are four of these narrow maskers either side of stage, each made of black cloth stretched over a thin steel frame. Two strides forward and I'm visible to the audience. I feel heat from the lights blazing away on the vertical boom arm behind and above. An identical set across stage shines directly in my eyes. During the quieter moments I hear the thump of the dancers' feet.

The music increases in volume, rises to a volatile crescendo. An abrupt end, then a great noise of fast clapping.

Heavy drapes smack the floor with a slight clink from the chain in the bottom which prevents them billowing. Auditorium claps and cheers become muffled. Rain falling on a cathedral roof. Relief is tangible. Our world is private, secure for a moment. Centre stage, Adele relaxes, professional demeanour, her character, allowed to depart for a few seconds.

Stand by! someone shouts and then Adele straightens, transforms once again into character just as the drapes fly out and the roar of the crowd increases.

THEY HAVE BEEN REHEARSING PROKOFIEV'S *ROMEO AND JULIET* FOR THE FOUR-WEEK tour of the US. Everyone has become very intense. The word going around is that it could be the season which propels Adele to international stardom. She has reached the age where, as a dancer, she is beginning to control things, to master her art.

We have been seeing a lot less of each other lately. Understandable, I suppose, considering she leads such a busy life. Wouldn't want to get in the way of her career so I make an effort to be as flexible as possible. Yesterday morning, however, was the start of something. Something that leaves me cold.

Adele doesn't answer my calls. I think it's because of her usual hectic schedule, but as the day progresses and I still can't get hold of her I begin to wonder if anything is wrong. I drive over to the theatre and manage to squeeze some information out of Dean. Though he seems very cagey. He says her parents are coming to see her before she flies to New York and she hasn't had time for anything. I sense something isn't right.

One of the girls in black tells me Adele is asleep in her dressing room, exhausted, and should not be disturbed. I decide to go for coffee in the cafeteria. On the way past reception I hear my name mentioned so I stop and listen, out of view. A rasping voice with a slight French tinge. Talking to Dean.

We all must play our part, Madame is saying. We are a family. Ballet is hard! Painful. Like life. We make painful decisions. Yes I contacted her parents. We are in agreement. It is for the best. They too must discourage her from seeing that man. We all should. He is not right for her. He is a loser! He has no *passion*!

I'm not sure I like this, Dean says.

You will do as you're told! croaks Madame. Otherwise you look for another position. Adele is responding already. She is losing interest in that chump. I think she has an eye for Carlo. Carlo is a good match. By the time we get back from America this problem will be resolved.

AFTER MUCH THOUGHT AND PAINFUL SELF-ANALYSIS, MY INITIAL FEELING IS THAT Madame is right. I'm not the man for Adele. I have nothing going for me whatsoever. She should be seeing some great-looking rich celebrity, an actor or sports star, someone like that. They would make a golden couple, feature in those society gossip mags. The publicity would benefit her career. There can be no doubt I am holding her back. That's how I felt at first.

After a sleepless week of being ripped apart inside, I arise one morning asking some simple questions. Anger surfaces. What if Adele is waiting for me to make a move? What if this is some kind of test to see if I'm worthy of such an incredible woman? Can I live the rest of my life with regrets, without ever knowing? One thing is for sure, the guy that wins Adele won't be the guy with his head stuck in the sand.

While Adele is in New York I sign up with a gym. I begin to eat the right foods, cut out alcohol, swap T-shirt and jeans for expensive shirt and trousers. I sit down to a video of *The Graduate*. I love that scene at the end when the entire bus is staring, the whole world against them, and they just look at each other and smile because they know they have something pure that nobody else can steal or corrupt. Dustin Hoffman's persistence gives me the kick up the arse I need. I decide to confront Madame. If it's a fight she wants, she's going to get it.

A PIANO REHEARSAL. APART FROM THE CLANKING PIANO THE THEATRE IS RELATIVELY quiet. No technicians, stage management or musicians around. This afternoon

I watch from the fly tower so I don't get noticed.

Adele is a grown woman. How dare Madame try to take control of her personal life, interfere with her happiness? I'm positive Adele loves me. That's why I must fight to keep her. Okay, so Madame has turned everyone against me — even Dean. But then no one said it was going to be easy.

Alone with my thoughts, I lean on the steel rail until I feel it pinching my elbows. The fly tower is a narrow walkway approximately ten metres above the stage. Madame, the pianist, Adele, and the male principal Carlo rehearse below me. At four o'clock Madame calls a break and they leave the stage.

Behind, running the length of the gantry, is a row of vertical ropes. Lever brakes release the ropes when the operator needs to move any scenery, which is suspended above the stage and hangs directly in front of me. Numerous loops and twists of electrical cables, huge square cloths, gauzes, and long steel pipes supporting dozens of black and chrome lamps. A good place to hide up here. Nice and dark.

Footsteps. Dean strolls across stage with some costumes. I'd like to speak to him but I don't want anyone to know I'm here. I'd rather there wasn't a scene. Prefer to catch Madame when no one else is around. Dean stops, looks up.

Did I make a noise? Is he looking for me? Surely it's too dark for him to see anything. He hangs the costumes on a rail, wanders out of view. I hear the swing of an exit door.

I decide to explore my surroundings a bit. A steel ladder, bolted to the wall, leads from the stage to the fly tower and then up to the roof about twenty metres above me. No harm in having a look.

At the top of the ladder I have to stretch my leg out and manoeuvre myself onto a small jutting platform. I step onto the platform, keeping my head low because of the angle of the roof beams. Careful to keep my concentration because it's quite a way down.

There must be a light switch somewhere but I don't bother looking. My eyes soon adjust to the gloom. This area is known as the grid, and supports the flown scenery. Like a giant attic really, except there are pulleys and steel wires everywhere, some electric motors and chain hoists. The floor is made of wooden slats, each about two centimetres apart, wide enough to see the stage far below. Adele and the others haven't returned from their break yet.

I find myself longing to see her again, just for a moment. A glimpse will do. Adele has become so much a part of my world now I can't imagine what I used to do before we met. A shallow unfulfilled existence. I was incomplete, emotionally undeveloped.

A noise. An arc of light cuts through darkness briefly as a door opens and closes. Someone is walking across the fly tower below, past where I was standing a couple of minutes ago. Probably a technician.

But then why hasn't he turned on the light?

The person stops, remains still, as if listening. He walks across to the foot of the ladder below me and stops again. Then he starts to climb to the grid.

What am I going to say? I think frantically for an excuse for my presence up here.

The fact he hasn't turned on the light makes me nervous. I'm still quite close to the ladder. I could try and hide but if I move he's sure to hear me. He's almost at the top. A leg stretches over to the platform. A hand appears, a head, ducking low. It's Dean. In the darkness it takes a moment for him to recognise me. "You!" he says. "You sick fuck!"

Once he's seen it's me he decides to retreat back down the ladder. But he's too slow. Must have been up partying last night. Drunk a bit too much red wine, smoked a couple of joints. As he steps off the platform I thrust my leg out. Boot catches him on the shoulder. Clumsy scuffing effort really, yet effective enough to cause him to lose his balance and his grip. He lets out a little gasp as he realises he's about to hurtle thirty metres to a hardwood floor.

BACKSTAGE DURING A BALLET REALLY IS A WONDERFUL EXPERIENCE. THE SILK BACK-drops and fine gauzes that, when lit in the colours of the forest, create a land of wonder and shadow, a faerie kingdom. The girls, unlike the boozy lumps down my local, are feminine and slight. They dress in pure white, giggle like elves, and when they pass you in the corridor the scent of wildflowers lingers. Is it surprising that I am addicted to this world?

I have watched Adele perform hundreds of times, in lots of different venues from Manchester to Milan. Recently, at one of my favourite theatres — a quaint old Victorian building of faded grandeur, with maroon velour seats and peeling walls — I walk along the corridor after finding Adele's dressing room and bump into Dean.

It had been simple enough to gain entry. Managed to stroll past the stage door attendant without getting noticed. The entrance backstage is always locked with a security code but from outside in the street, through the window, it's possible to see people tapping in the four numbers. So that's what I did. Easy.

Adele is in number one dressing room. Figures. She's quite a star these days. I love the fragrance of her rooms. I linger, I savour. I lose all sense of time. At some point instinct tells me I must leave. On the way out I close the door quietly.

Dean is standing there, puzzled. "Can I help? Are you looking for someone?"

"Uh . . . no," I say, staring at the floor. "I'm okay thanks." At such times I have no confidence. Always been like that. Words lodge in my throat and can find no release. I feel my face flush.

"Are you crew? I've seen you around . . ."

Sticking out of my pocket is a black lace-trim thong. Dean spots it before I have a chance to stuff it in properly.

Certainty sharpens his features. "*You're* the one who's been sending her those letters, aren't you?" he says. "Now I understand."

I try to speak. To put into words my love for Adele. Impossible. If only Dean could understand how I felt the night I spoke with her. During that first-night party I gatecrashed. I will never forget those few seconds as long as I live.

"She's very precious to us," Dean says, distressed now, almost tearful. "We love her very much."

"So do I," I manage to shout. The corridor echoes with the conviction of my soul.

"I'm calling the police."

I follow him back to stage door. Past reception I hear him on the phone saying all sorts of nasty things about me. Words like 'stalker', 'deluded' and 'psycho'.

I used to imagine that one day Dean would be my only friend. Now he's gone and spoiled all that.

Anyway, I go back a couple of days later and watch a piano rehearsal from the fly tower. That's when Dean has his little fall. He collides with the metal rail on his way down to stage. Very nasty. Adele and the others find him making a horrid wheezing sound. Maybe he was trying to tell them something, and all that came out was frothing blood. Amazing how durable the human body is. Dean survives for thirty minutes and dies in the ambulance. Massive head and internal injuries. Basically, his insides were pulped; leaking from every orifice. The local paper said it was an accident. Although nobody can understand what Dean was doing up there in the grid. Such are the mysteries of life.

FOLLOWING ADELE AROUND IS AN EXPENSIVE BUSINESS. I'M SURVIVING OFF SAVINGS after my business went under three months ago. One of my fantasies is landing a job with a firm that sponsors her ballet company. A gateway to her world.

I couldn't afford the recent trip to New York. At first I was devastated but then I realised the situation's potential. I broke into Adele's apartment and slept in her bed for two nights. I snatched her bedding and replaced it with an identical set. Naughty boy. It will never be washed. Our dead skin and body hair shall remain as one.

We *will* be lovers. Okay, so she may not be aware of that yet but I feel I'm getting closer to her all the time. I know so much about her, so many fine details, it's easy to include her in my world. Her pictures cover my bedroom walls. I lie on the mattress staring at them and in no time Adele is curled up next to me. I drape her unwashed sheets over me and sit like that for hours.

At the local pub I get the feeling people don't take me seriously. At first they just found me a bore. Now I've become a figure of fun.

"When are you going to bring your girlfriend round then?" they say, laughing. An exchange of looks, alluding to previous discussions, no doubt. "You going to buy her a pint when she comes Harvey?"

"She drinks white wine," I say. "Only one glass with soda if she's performing next night."

They laugh some more. "Living in a fantasy world!" someone says. "Fucking weirdo!"

"I've got these," I say, producing a black lace thong from my pocket. "Now aren't they special?"

THE BEAUTIFUL BALLERINA SMILES IN A CURIOUS, INQUISITIVE MANNER. MY HEART quickens as she makes her way over. Small feet direct outwards slightly — the result of years of forced stances and painful contortions. Gives the impression of effortless gliding, and makes her even more attractive to me. I'm flattered when she introduces herself and chats away as if we've known each other for years. Even more flattered when she suggests I go back to her apartment for a drink.

Any ideas that her strong supple body may be a little overtired after such a rigorous stage workout are soon dispelled. I collapse in a sweating tangle at 4AM, craving sleep, barely noticing the tugging at my elbow, the hungry voice in my ear. *Please* Harvey, she whispers. Do it one more time.

My life begins.

stasi-17

ceri jordan

Ceri Jordan lives in mid-Wales. After
many years as an SF and dark fantasy
writer, she was lured into crime
(fiction, or so she claims) by the
promise of cash. She has recently sold
her first film script, and is glad to
report that in the film industry, there
really is such a thing as a free lunch.

THE NIGHT TRAIN EAST FROM MUNICH WAS LESS A MEANS OF TRANSPORT, MORE A hotel on wheels. No room service — no rooms, just a seat if you were lucky and the corridor if not. And people. Turks, skinheads, skateboarders and businessmen shoulder to shoulder, engaged in the well-practised art of ignoring one another's walkmans, elbows, and body odour. And everywhere, the faint sounds of sleep. Shivers, shudders, grunts and moans, mingling with the rattle of loose windows and the continual tinnitus-sounds of the public address system.

Last time Tom had made this journey, back in The Bad Old Days, the train had been all but deserted. But then, the last time he'd made this journey, he'd been armed and had money and a passport, and hadn't spent half an hour scrubbing blood from his shirt cuffs, and in retrospect, The Bad Old Days weren't looking so bad any more.

1AM. They'd be pulling into Essendorf any minute. Sleeping travellers groaned in unison as the train slowed, sensing another thirty-second halt in another dead-end town, resenting the delay.

The only other passenger awake was a young Turkish woman, headscarfed but not veiled, arm in arm with a sleeping man whom Tom hoped was her grandfather. It had been just her and him for a while now, stubborn resistors in a carriage that seemed to be under the effect of chloroform. He wondered what her reasons were, why she couldn't close her eyes and let go. He hoped they were less urgent than his.

The station lights swung into view as they lurched round the final corner. Tom stood up. The nearest door was behind him, but something made him turn the other way, pick his way over sleeping teenagers towards the headscarfed woman.

She watched him incuriously until he drew level, and then turned her head to study the platform decelerating beside them. He felt a sudden desperate urge to speak to her. To see her nod or smile or shrink away in panic. To establish that he still had a place in the real world.

But his mouth was dry and the train was almost stationary, and instead he hugged his coat tighter around himself and moved silently to the door.

THE WIND WAS FIERCE, AND THE PAVEMENTS SPARKLED WITH A TREACHEROUS FROST. Suppressing a moment's grief for the loss of his thick camel coat — irretrievably stained with his attacker's blood, and abandoned in favour of a trench coat stolen from the back of a chair — Tom crossed into the shelter of a row of shops.

A single taxi lingered at the station, its internal lights bright in the gathering mist. He might have enough for the fare to Mac's, but it would be unwise. Taxi drivers remembered faces, particularly late fares with paranoid eyes and half-developed bruises, and a few marks would generally buy the details and the delivery address.

He'd have to walk.

Essendorf was a sad, grey little place. The road led past a few corner shops to a cobbled square dominated by a heavy-set town hall in weather-beaten stone. As he headed south, into a stretch of boutique shops, headlights glazed the windows ahead. He moved sideways, into the shadow of the nearest building.

It was the taxi from the station. In the dark interior, only the pinpoint glow of a cigarette gave away the presence of a passenger. For a moment, he thought it was slowing, and scanned the street for an alleyway, a fire escape, anywhere a vehicle couldn't follow. But it jolted from cobbles to Tarmac and accelerated again, taking the next right and fading audibly into the distance.

The boutiques gave way to unfamiliar ground — a new shopping area, sparkling department stores with familiar names. The tidal wave of prosperity that the collapse of the Wall was supposed to unleash had washed over Essendorf, but it had left little in its wake. Further down the now-pedestrianised precinct, the shops became tackier, cheaper, and finally became empty windows and FOR RENT signs.

Disoriented by progress, Tom emerged through market stalls into a narrow, winding street. The ground fell away sharply towards the river, visible as a thick band of white mist beyond the receding rooftops. Schweinstrasse. That was right. Fourth on the left; a red door between two rundown bars, ring the bell three times, wait, once, wait, once again.

If Mac's still here. If he can be trusted. Everything an 'if'.

Just like The Bad Old Days.

He rang the code with the precision of long practise, and waited.

Finally, the door creaked open, and a familiar voice murmured from the darkness, "Tom. How nice to see you. Love the coat."

THE MAIN ROOM HAD BEEN PAINTED, A PALE GREEN THAT SAT UNEASILY WITH THE luminous orange sofa, but nothing else had changed. Avoiding low-flying wind-chimes, Tom scooped an armful of American magazines 'for the gun enthusiast' from the nearest armchair, and slumped into it.

The kettle clicked on, and Mac emerged from the tiny kitchen area, ducking the lintel. He'd always looked out of scale in the flat, a giant squeezed into a world of the average.

"Well," he said. "Tom Whelan. How very . . . unexpected."

"Is this place secure?"

Mac smiled. "Well, that answers my question about whether you're still in the trade."

"I'm serious, Mac. Is this place secure?"

"Yes, it's secure. Probably more so than it was last time you were here. My new line of business pays rather better."

Willing his trembling hands to steady, Tom sat back in the armchair. "Okay. Mac. It's good to see you, and everything, but I need your help."

"Yes," Mac muttered, the remains of his Scots burr strengthening. "I rather thought this wasn't a social call. What happened?"

"I was on a job in Slovakia, and it . . . went wrong. I had an escape route to Hamburg, I took it, and when I got there . . ." He closed his eyes, willing the memories back into the darkness. "The safe house was already in enemy hands. I gave the right code, they let me in . . . I barely got out with my life. Lost everything. Passport, most of my cash."

"Any ideas who?"

"Islamic extremists. Judging from why I was in Slovakia. Spoke Arabic. I didn't stop to take notes."

The kettle's hiss became a click, then silence. Mac chewed absently on his lower lip. "I sincerely hope," he murmured, "that you weren't followed here."

"I'm as sure as I can be."

"Bugs?"

"I stole a suitcase, changed most of my clothes. Bought new shoes. Washed my hair."

"You always were efficient," Mac conceded, heading back to the kitchen.

"Comes of working with the best."

Mac didn't reply.

Tom sat for a moment, letting the trembling in his legs subside. It was leaking back in, now he was safe. Everything he'd pushed out of his mind for the past twenty-four hours. The shock, the exhaustion, the pain of torn muscles and bruised flesh. Another half hour and he'd be out; asleep, or as good as.

Stay focused. Get an answer.

Be sure you're safe.

He went to the window, opened the heavy curtains a crack, using his body to minimize the amount of light escaping. The street was empty, the windows opposite mostly shuttered.

"Not entirely sure you weren't followed, then," Mac observed dryly.

"Like I said, sure as I can be." Folding the curtains carefully back into place, Tom returned to his seat. A mug of black coffee had materialised on the teak table beside it, accompanied by a thick, no-nonsense sandwich. White bread and pale ham, greased with mustard.

"So, you want my help."

Mouth full, Tom settled for a casual shrug.

Mac smiled again. Either the past decade had softened him, or he was in a spectacularly good mood. "We're old friends, you and I. Comrades bound together by the trials of war, and all that poetic shite. I'd help you just because of that — you know that, or you'd never have come here."

"You know the Department will pay you back. Cash, favours — "

"Actually, I was hoping for a favour from you." Holding up a hand to silence Tom's protests, he continued, "You see, your arrival here, now, is terribly convenient. So much so that, under any other circumstances, I'd have assumed it was a trap and broken your neck the moment you walked through the door."

Knowing better than to protest innocence, or anything else, Tom sipped coffee, and waited.

"But as I said, we're old friends. And you always took that seriously. Oh, if I turned against the country, betrayed the Department, you'd take me down in an instant. But if I choose to live abroad and engage in a little casual gunrunning to suitably distant countries . . . that's none of your business. Right?"

Tom nodded.

"Good. Let's talk terms. You have knowledge and skills I need. I can arrange a passport, money, clothing. A halfway decent haircut would be a start . . . You help me do one job, and I get you safely home. Deal?"

He knows you're going to ask. It's in his eyes, the beginnings of a smile pushing at the corners of his mouth, in the way he's looking at you over his espresso cup. He knows you won't commit to this blind, and he loves you for it. 'What's the job, Mac?'

Staring across at him in the yellow lamplight, Mac said softly, "I need you to get me into Stasi-17."

HE DREAMED THAT NIGHT.

He hadn't dreamed for years, not this dream: but tonight, curled in the treacherous embrace of the overstuffed sofa, it returned with a vengeance.

Like an old TV programme, the plot varied but the opening was always the same. First the cold. Starting in his toes, his fingers. He has to turn over, curl up, conserve heat, but he can't. The wire cuts into his ankles, slips inexorably deeper into the raw wounds marking his wrists.

He can hear the night coming. The banal chatter of guards going off shift, passing his door on the way to changing rooms and showers and exits. The small sounds of security systems activating, the hum of sensor systems warming up in empty corridors.

He's pinned like a butterfly in the killing jar, and any time now the night shift come on duty and the bolt on the door will slide back and the light leak in as they enter —

"HERR WHELAN?"

His hand moved of its own accord. Brain a few a few vital seconds behind, lagging to process the fact it was a woman's voice, the light was all wrong, and anyway, why were his hands free if — ?

He froze.

The girl standing over him looked down at the stiffened fingers poised millimetres from her throat, and shook her head. "He's slow," she said.

"He's tired," Mac observed, somewhere across the room. "Run halfway across Europe to get here. He'll sharpen up in a few hours. Coffee, Tom? And a little light breakfast, perhaps?"

"You should have gone into the hotel trade, Mac. I always said you were wasted in procurement."

The girl shook her head again. Now he looked closer, behind the scraped-back dark hair and the immaculate make-up, she barely looked old enough to be wandering round an arms dealer's flat at this time in the morning. Whatever time it was.

"So," Tom managed, suddenly aware that he was stark naked and the quilt, dislodged by his attempt at self-defence, was barely covering his embarrassment. "Good morning. And you are . . . ?"

"You'd *better* sharpen up," she murmured. "I said I'd do this if Mac found a way in. I said nothing about striking deals with a washed-up covert operative with bad reflexes."

"And I didn't sign up for Essendorf High, kid. Looks like we'll all have to improvise."

She moved away, across the flat. To Mac, no doubt. To protest or wheedle or kiss. Bloody Mac and his bloody skill at pulling teenagers . . .

Folding the quilt around himself, Tom sat up.

Translucent blinds covered the street-facing windows, filtering the sunlight to a milky glow. The kitchen window was open, admitting musty air, distant traffic sounds, and a view of the river and the leafy suburbs on the far bank.

"What time is it?"

"4PM. There are clean clothes in the bathroom, and a shaving kit. Lucy was kind enough to go shopping for you." Amusement coloured his voice. "Say 'Thank you, Lucy."

"Yeah. Thanks, Lucy." Shoving the quilt aside, Tom levered himself to his feet and swayed towards the bathroom door. "I'm eternally grateful. The Department's eternally grateful. No doubt Mac is eternally grateful too, Mac and his crackpot scheme — "

To break into Stasi-17.

Kicking the door closed behind him, Tom leant over the immaculate porcelain basin, took a firm hold on the gold-plated taps, and threw up.

6PM EXACTLY, THE DOORBELL RANG. THREE RINGS, A GAP, THREE RINGS. WATCHING Mac's broad shoulders disappear through the door to the stairs, Tom wondered if he'd reassigned their old code ring to one of his new associates. Whether he'd opened the door last night expecting to find a contact or a buyer, instead of an old friend with half of Islam hot on his heels.

Lucy strode from the kitchen, set down a heavy Turkish style coffee pot and a tray of tiny china cups. That, and a dented leather folio bursting with papers and architectural drawings, took up most of the dining table.

"Can I help with anything?"

She shook her head. Vanished again; returned with milk and sugar in tiny silver containers, crafted to match the pot. Typical Mac. He'd always had too much taste for a covert.

Their supervisor claimed she'd had Mac marked as 'vulnerable' from day one, but the honey-traps and the envelopes of money had come his way and he'd rejected them all. Kept his head down, learned the trade, and took one of the first voluntary redundancies the Department had ever seen. They'd laughed about it over a brandy in Vienna, the day after the paperwork came through. What was he going to tell them down the Job Centre? He'd spent the last twelve years saving the world, now he wanted a nice part-time number with a good retirement package?

Lucy's fingers brushed Tom's shoulder, returning him abruptly to reality. He looked up.

"You're cold?"

He fingered the weave of the pullover himself, aware that the gesture somehow linked them. Soft cotton in a rich spice brown, subtle and flattering. He imagined her standing over the sofa as he slept, noting his complexion, selecting a colour palette.

"Be ungrateful not to wear it," he said. "After you bought it. I mean."

Smiling thinly, she sat down opposite him. Though the sun was low now, the kitchen blinds flapping in a gathering breeze, she still wore a tight short-sleeved top and jeans. A tangle of bracelets, metal and jade, rattled on her wrist. He had a sudden vision of those bracelets pressing into his bruised flesh as her hands moved over his body, and drew breath sharply.

The door creaked open behind him, admitting Mac's voice. "A new recruit — a very lucky break indeed . . ."

"We can conduct this meeting in German," Tom observed, pretending an interest in the embossed spine of the folio, the coffee pot, anything but Lucy.

"Actually, no." Mac indicated for the new arrivals to take their seats. "Mr Greenlea here doesn't speak German."

"Regrettably," Mr Greenlea rumbled, lowering himself into the chair beside Tom. New York twang, immaculately tailored jacket. A small player trying his luck on new territory: eager, hungry, dangerous. Just the kind of man Mac liked to deal with.

The other arrival, a small man with one permanently drooping eyelid, extended a hand. "Gunther," he conceded. "So, what skill has Mac recruited you for? Don't tell me you're a police officer?"

"Not . . . exactly."

"Tom's experience of this facility rather predates the involvement of the police." Sitting down, Mac opened the folio, retrieved a blueprint and spread it on the table. With the speed of long practise, Lucy snatched the coffee pot away an instant before he knocked it over.

"To summarise: four days ago, the ever vigilant local police finally managed to seize a truckload of goods destined for my store in Dussburg. Mostly firearms and ammo, some explosives. They have impounded it, with admirable irony, in a secure depot beneath the hydroelectric plant up-river at Godensdorf. That part of the depot was once secretly used by the Stasi for interrogating valuable prisoners. It was secure — thought inescapable — and no one was around to hear the screams. We, with our wonderful British sense of humour, used to call it Stasi-17."

No one saw fit to even smile.

"In a recent interview, the head of the facility admitted that they were still using the state of the art security system the Stasi installed — excessive for their current needs, but why waste it? After all, only one man ever got past it."

Lucy raised her gaze to Tom's, her eyes soft with understanding.

"Only one prisoner ever escaped from Stasi-17, gentlemen — and he is sitting at this table right now. His way out will be our way in . . . " Mac showed his teeth, the smile that Tom knew wasn't a smile at all. "As soon as he sees fit to share it with us."

"YOU DON'T NEED ME," TOM ANNOUNCED, AFTER THEIR CO-CONSPIRATORS HAD gone and the flat was silent again. "You could walk in the front door with an AK, lock up the guards, take the goods and go."

The daylight was almost gone, and Lucy had turned on all the table lamps before retreating up the foldaway ladder to the attic bedroom. Mac was carefully filing the folio and loose papers back onto a groaning bookshelf. Many of the adjacent folders had Departmental code names, and not all of them dated from Mac's period of employment. There was something to mention to the desk-job-boys, if he ever got home . . .

"Oh, we'd have gone in somehow or other," Mac conceded. "But since you're here, we may as well make use of you. A covert entry will increase the time we have to load the truck." His hand fell heavily on Tom's shoulder as he passed, startling him. "And I've always wondered how a mediocre by-the-book spook like you pulled off that stunt. Chapman always insisted you bought your way out. A thousand US dollars in your shoe lining, that's your sort of safety net, isn't it?"

Keeping his tone light, Tom observed, "Three hundred, actually. But they took my shoes."

"Not just the laces, the whole shoe? That's the Stasi for you. Nothing if not efficient." His fingers gripped Tom's shoulder for a moment longer, then lifted. Tom heard the creak of the staircase as he ascended towards the attic. "Looks like I was right all along. You sucked every cock that was offered to you until you found the man with the key. We leave at ten. Stay away from the windows. Gunther, bigoted fellow that he is, says the town's just crawling with Turks today."

Tom closed his eyes. Distant rock music merged with the chatter of schoolgirls in the street, and the muffled endearments echoing in the hollow arches of the attic. When the whispers gave way to grunts and giggles and cries, he went out to the kitchen and stood watching the sunset and the blue flicker of TV in distant windows, weighing his options.

If he could make it to somewhere crowded, a bar or a club, he could get money. Handbags, coat pockets, all easy pickings. Then the train station — or better still, hotwire a reliable car and head south. There was a driver at the embassy in Paris who could get a message to the Department, and French/German passport controls were pretty much nonexistent now . . .

If he made it out of Essendorf.

Upstairs, Lucy had finally fallen silent. It occurred to him, without surprise, that Mac hadn't made a sound.

Another big 'if'. He'd been lucky to get out of Slovakia, and Hamburg had been a bloody miracle. A third attempt would be pushing his luck quite severely.

He opened the cupboards, moving round the kitchen until he found the inevitable bottle of single malt, and half-filled a tumbler.

Stasi-17. God help us all.

Down in the street, a young woman in a white headscarf glanced up at him as he raised the glass, and looked quickly away.

"It was the woman from the train."

"For God's sake, Tom. What is the likelihood — "

"That she's a pavement artist for the bastards who've been chasing me for the last forty-eight hours? Quite high, wouldn't you say?"

Mac shook his head irritably. "Well, considering how well Lucy has taken to the art of defensive driving, I think we can assume we've shaken her."

Glancing back at the dark hump of the BMW, where Lucy was unloading their kit, Tom conceded, "Oh, she's a woman of many talents, your Lucy. You brought the equipment?"

"Gunther will bring it."

"Why aren't they here?"

"They'll show." Mac bit his lip. "If you have anything to confess, Tom, now would be the time."

Even quietly spoken to an innocent man, the words made him shiver. "Such as?"

"Such as: there is no escape route. You bribed your way out, with money or information. You wouldn't be the first — and they were rough on you, I saw the medical files . . ."

Closing his eyes for a moment, summoning back the memories he'd spent years drowning in alcohol and work and psychobabble, Tom murmured, "You'd like that, wouldn't you?"

"Under any other circumstances, I'd laugh until I fell over. But since that's my property they have down there . . ."

"You'll get your way in, Mac. I just hope you're up to it."

Headlights flickered behind them, glancing from the few stunted trees topping the ridge, then vanished as the car turned onto the dirt track behind them.

"Mr Greenlea." Even in the dark, he could feel Mac's smile. "I hope."

Tom walked away.

The slope was shallow; as his eyes adjusted, he could make out beer cans, bait boxes, the firefly delicacy of abandoned fishing tackle. A hundred yards away, the reservoir lay mirror-smooth and silent, reflecting back a few isolated stars.

He could feel the vibration hum of the turbines already. The hum he'd felt in every muscle for weeks, months after the escape, the hum that still filled the quiet hours between the nightmares and dawn. He thought of it as memory; the distilled memories of every scream, every tear, every despairing, unnoticed death at 2AM that had ever occurred down there. All the memories that had only been able to escape in him.

Clouds rolled overhead, turning the water to black velvet. Below, Stasi-17 waited in the dark for him, as it had done every night for twelve years.

"WELL," GUNTHER ANNOUNCED, AS TOM ASCENDED THE SLOPE TO JOIN THEM. "Beautiful night for it. I have the kebab sticks, I hope you remembered the barbecue . . ."

"Show me."

Gunther handed him a plastic pack: a good label, expensive. A dozen metal meat skewers, steel. Exactly what he'd asked for.

"Have any of you ever climbed?"

"A little," Lucy offered. "My dad took me. Mac?"

"He knows I can climb, my dear. We once went up three thousand feet of snowbound crevasse, with ten pounds of plastique each and supplies for a week. What exactly he thinks we're going to climb out here — "

"Mr Greenlea?"

"I've climbed walls plenty of times. Roofs, gutters. No mountains, though." He showed his teeth in a thin smile. "No mountains in Watts."

"Sounds like you'll make it. Gunther?"

The small man shook his head. "I will be staying here. Well, in fact, I will be towing Mac's car back into town, before the alarms go off and the police search the area."

Greenlea frowned slightly. "All right, we're climbing. But what?"

Following the direction of his gaze, Tom shook his head. "Not the dam, no. Or I'd have told you to bring your swimming trunks."

No laughter. Drawing breath for the explanation, he felt a twinge of regret, even guilt. This was his secret, the one he'd only shared with his immediate superiors, the one only a few classified documents recorded. The one achievement Mac hadn't ever equalled, demeaned, or stolen from him.

"Stasi-17 is on the other side of the river, built into the side of the hill. Under the hydroelectric plant. There's a road entrance — heavily guarded — and there are emergency staircases up to the plant. That's how we go in. But first we have to get inside the wall of the dam, and through the plant. Which at night is totally automated — and riddled with motion sensors. Anything that moves triggers an alarm."

Mac met his gaze steadily. Waiting for the revelation.

"Anything that moves at ground level, anyway."

A SMEAR OF PLASTIQUE TOOK THE LOCK OFF THE EMERGENCY HATCH, AND THEY lined up along the shore to watch as Tom descended.

Darkness, cold concrete on all sides. His own height, further. For the first time, it occurred to him that the rope ladder might not be long enough. He should have thought of that. It was the part he'd already done that had taken up all his worrying time. This initial part, the part he'd improvised to cover the ignominious end to his escape, he'd barely considered.

Another step, and grey light showed him his own feet.

Gripping the edge of the ladder with both hands, Tom drew his knees up to his chest. Somewhere out in the wind, he could hear Mac cursing. Tightening his stomach muscles, he tipped his head back — gingerly, aware of the walls pressing in — and raised his knees. Straightened his legs. Upside down now, feet hooked onto a rung, working his way down with his hands.

He ached already.

Headfirst into the corridor, cramp-ridden and defenceless.

The hum swallowed his senses; the hum, the cold, the grey grimy light. The smell. He'd forgotten the smell — oil and metal and rancid water, the smell of abandoned canals and the skeletons of cars.

Seven feet below him, the dim red lines of sensor beams crisscrossed the corridor like drawn swords. Ten feet, perhaps twelve, of sensor protection, then the floor. Concrete. Headfirst onto that, he wouldn't be answering any questions when the security guards got there anyway.

Freeing one leg, he braced his foot against the mouth of the hatchway and turned to survey his escape route.

The corridor was huge. Twenty feet square, built to accommodate repair equipment on a grand scale. Something on treads waited halfway down the corridor, the top of its cab protruding out of the danger zone. That would make a good rest stop. If they could get that far.

Every ten feet, a curve of concrete and steel joined wall and ceiling, supporting the weight of the solid dam with a web of Art Deco swirls.

His collar microphone was dangling in midair; he had to shift position to be sure the others would hear. "I'm going to fix the end of the ladder to a buttress to the right of the hatch. As long as nothing you're carrying protrudes below the line of the ladder, you'll be safe."

"Hurry it along, Tom," Mac's voice growled in his earpiece. "Your acrobatics are terribly amusing, but it is rather getting cold up here."

Sighing heavily, Tom lowered himself another five rungs, and swung his weight forward.

Back, forward, back; leaning into it, building momentum. The lines of red light below swirled into dizzying patterns, intersecting and separating. The thin metal arch of the roof buttress lurched into his field of vision, vanished. Reappeared. For longer. Another push, an inch more reach —

His hand closed over the blunt edge of the girder. Wrenched to a dead stop, he gasped, had to fight instinct to maintain his grip. Pain flooded his shoulder, triggering twinges of sympathy from old bruises.

Fine, you're in pain. You were in worse when you got out of this place. And this time you have kit, and a gun, and if Mac's in a really trusting mood, the ammo in your clip might even be live . . .

Feeling his way to the trailing end of the ladder, Tom took a firm grip and disentangled his feet. Keeping his knees drawn up, everything above sensor height. Right. Just attach the ladder to the buttress — two loops of safety cord each side, always be sure — and you can climb up into the metalwork and rest . . .

His back to the wall, hugging the decorative arch of the buttress like a lover, Tom whispered, "All right, Mac. Come join the party."

LUCY CAME FIRST, CROSSING THE SHIFTING ROPE BRIDGE LIKE A CHILD ON A CLIMB-ing frame. Greenlea followed more cautiously, and spent far too much time looking down.

When Mac finally joined them, quick as a monkey, hooking himself into the few remaining handholds on the buttress with an expert's precision, Tom was already showing the others how to bend their metal skewers.

"An angle of about forty-five degrees. Good. Now take the rope loops, hitch them through the loop on the end of the skewer. When you're not using it, keep the loop round your wrist."

Tugging experimentally on the length of rope, Lucy observed, "There must be something better than this. Climbing equipment."

"I used a skewer. I know it'll work."

"Used it," Greenlea rumbled, "to do what?"

Pointing past them to the ceiling, Mac muttered, "That."

The dam's designers hadn't gone to much trouble to hide the metal superstructure. Here, girders showed in the ceiling like the ribs of the starving, smooth and impossible to grip. The only imperfection were the bolt holes. Too narrow for a hold, even a single finger.

Reaching up to the first hole, Tom slotted the bent skewer into it and tugged. Secure.

Mac shook his head wearily. "And for this, they gave you a commendation."

"I don't get it," Greenlea muttered. "Where'd you get a kebab skewer in a police cell?"

Second skewer into a hole a good arm's length away; pushing off from his foothold, Tom cautiously lowered his legs. A good twelve inches clearance above the sensors.

"I broke an ankle strap. Kicked my interrogator in the nuts."

And swing for the next hold. The skewer slots home. See, it's easy . . .

"One of the guards went down to the kitchen and came back with meat skewers. And a lump hammer. They hammered them through my lower legs, bent the ends over to hold me."

And release, swing forward, hook, redistribute your weight, and here's the next buttress . . .

"Good thing I did figure out this route out. Using my arms, mostly. I couldn't have walked more than a few yards."

And when I got lost and fell into a turbine out-take, I couldn't use my legs and almost drowned.

Slotting his leg through an ornate metal curve, Tom looked back at them. Greenlea looked like he was about to be sick. Mac, studiously unimpressed, was already leaning out to find his first skewer-hold.

And Lucy was watching him with a slight, brittle pity, as if she'd heard all this somewhere before.

THEY RESTED ON THE CAB OF THE TRUCK FOR A WHILE, LISTENING TO THE TURBINE hum. Lucy handed round barley sugars from an inner pocket. Only Mac refused the offer. Staring down through the translucent roof at the controls, Tom found himself putting together a number of theories about her competence, and liking none of them.

Don't be ludicrous. Mac always picks practical women, and trains them to his purposes. You know that. Paranoia's setting in, and you can't afford it right now.

But you know there's something wrong here. You didn't just happen to attract fire at the precise moment Mac most needed you. And if it isn't Lucy or Greenlea pulling the strings . . .

"We should move," Mac said, standing up. "We don't have much time."

"We have all night," Tom observed. "I don't want anyone wearing themselves out. We have another hundred yards of corridor, then a crawl through a roof space to the first staircase — "

"We'll manage," Lucy said, heading off the argument. "Won't we?"

Greenlea flexed the muscles in his arms, winced. "I guess."

As Tom stood up, Mac nudged carelessly past him and murmured, "I'll lead the way now, thank you."

Emotions collided in Tom's head; anger, amusement, a vague rush of relief.

And yes, for the first time, a touch of certainty.

"Fine, Mac," he murmured, shifting the pistol inside his hip pocket. "You go right ahead."

IT WAS A TIGHT SCRAMBLE FROM THE FINAL BUTTRESS TO THE VENTILATOR SHAFT. Greenlea couldn't manage the foot jam, and in the end Tom had to hang off the ceiling, four skewers forced through the only useable hold, and grip him round the waist with both legs, swinging him at the open hatch like a parcel until Lucy and Mac pulled him in.

Sweat-drenched and shivering, Tom finally landed inside the shaft to find only Lucy still there.

"They went ahead."

"Which way?"

She nodded into the dark. "Ahead."

Prolonged effort had left him dizzy; lunging forward, he caught at her shoulder as she turned to follow them, barely gained a hold. "Don't play dumb with me. I know there's more going on here than he's said."

"I think," the girl said stiffly, "you should let me go."

"He knew I was coming. Didn't he?"

Her fingertips brushed his; gently, firmly, pried his hand from her shoulder. "Yes," she said. "And if we don't catch up with them soon, he'll know that you know. We're in, Tom. He doesn't need you now. Keep your head down, and he'll probably keep his promise. It's less effort for him than having to dispose of you. But if you cause him any trouble . . ."

Drying his hands on his jeans, Tom squinted into the dark. It wasn't that far to the hatch into the ceiling crawl-space. Mac was probably crouched there right now, listening in.

"He should think twice about whether he still needs me. He should know a professional never gives away the whole plan at once."

"Mmm," Lucy murmured, as he edged away into the dark. "And so should you."

IT TOOK THEM TIME TO FIND THE RIGHT DIRECTION; TIME, AND THE RISK OF LIFTING ceiling tiles here and there to peer into darkened rooms and get their bearings. Direction hadn't been important on the way out. He'd been running blind, struggling a few yards and then resting, always resting, praying for some miraculous restoration of his ability to walk, or even just to feel his legs —

Tom blinked.

The soft pop of a tile slotting back into place, shutting out the light, and Mac's voice growled, "The next room is the security office. Once we're in there, we can turn off the security precautions, and take the elevator down to the storage depot, two floors below."

Memory flickered: a cramped rectangular room, glimpsed as he was dragged to or from the desultory attentions of the Stasi's medical officer. "I'll go in first."

"That's very kind, Tom, but they're only civilian security. I think we'll manage to neutralise them."

"That," Tom murmured, "is exactly why I'm going in first."

Cold metal poked into the flesh of his cheek. "If I take the safety off this, Tom," Mac murmured, "the guards in there will almost certainly hear the click, and activate the alarms. And then I'll just have to pull the trigger."

"Go to hell."

"You didn't offer me the opportunity," Mac whispered, too soft for the others to hear. "You took off on that stupid recon mission without me, and you got yourself caught, and sent here. You went to hell without me, Tom, and you got out again and won all the medals and the praise, and I think that's when I realised that I really don't like you at all."

Keeping his breathing steady, Tom closed his eyes and waited for what was left of Mac's sanity to reassert itself.

The gun muzzle withdrew.

"Stay," Mac whispered.

The soft shuffle of bodies moving across metalwork and polystyrene, a rustle of clothing. Despite himself, he tensed. Then the crunch of shattering tiles, and a flood of light showed him Mac and Greenlea, plunging feet-first into a pit of flickering lights, cigarette smoke, and screams.

Three shots. A fourth. Polystyrene flowered upwards like snow, fluttered back through the gap. He heard the ricochet from the girder above them, lost track of where the round ended up.

At his shoulder, Lucy drew breath.

"Is this what you signed up for?" he asked her, more from malice than curiosity.

For answer, she pressed a fingertip briefly to his lips.

"Alarms are off," Mac called. "Come on down. You may want to cover your eyes, if you're feeling delicate."

"I'm fine," Lucy said stonily, edging quickly forward. Away from Tom.

Smiling up through the ragged gap in the ceiling, Mac assured her, "I know, my love. I wasn't talking to you."

THE ELEVATOR OPENED STRAIGHT INTO THE ENTRY HALL, A SPACE THE SIZE OF AN aircraft hangar hewn out of the bare rock. A row of floodlights about fifteen feet up filled the lower cavern with a low-voltage murk. The main lights, the ones he remembered from his ignominious arrival, were off, leaving the roof arch a pit of blackness.

Shielding his eyes against the uneven glare, Greenlea asked, "How much of this lot is yours?"

Mac strode forward into the empty roadway, surveying the parking area. Crammed with impounded trucks. GRAUBER'S IMPORT/EXPORT, EUROPIA FINE FOODS; pictures of happy grazing cows, animated wooden crates with toothy smiles, honesty and innocence.

Their contents had been removed, shrink-wrapped onto pallets and laid out behind them like organs arranged for an autopsy. Even with the peculiar underwater light silvering the wrappings, Tom could make out their contents. Rifles, subs, shotguns. Explosives, plastered with HANDLE WITH CARE! signs. Mortar launchers. Detonators, radios, electronics he couldn't name and didn't want to. All the way down to the little essentials: field kitchens, food rations, sacks of newly-dyed fatigues, mosquito killer. Every tin-pot dictator's idea of paradise.

"As much as we can get onto the three largest lorries," Mac beamed. "Mr Greenlea, I believe you said you could operate a forklift truck?"

"Sure." Rolling up his sleeves in an unnecessary display of eagerness, Greenlea headed towards the nearest forklift.

"Three trucks," Tom observed dryly, "and four drivers?"

"Now, now, Tom, don't get jumpy." Smooth as a diplomat again; no acknowledgement that five minutes ago he'd been pressing a gun muzzle into his dear old friend's face. "You'll be driving the first one out — and I'll be riding shotgun."

"Just like old times."

Mac smiled thinly. "Indeed. Lucy, my darling, you stay here and help Mr Greenlea load up. I'll trust his judgment as to what to take. Tom and I —" a hand fell on Tom's shoulder, spinning him back towards the elevator, " — will go back upstairs and pick up the star prize."

AS THE ELEVATOR STRAINED UPWARDS, THE INTERNAL LIGHTS DIMMING IN SYMPATHY with its struggles, Tom asked softly, "Is any of that stuff down there actually yours?"

"Some of it. But you don't think I would have taken this risk simply to steal back a few rifles, do you?"

"I think," Tom conceded, "there must be serious money involved somewhere here. You never were a risk-taker. Not unless the outcome was certain and the profits high."

"How cutting."

A moment, while Tom analysed his tone, judging how far to push him, and finally said, "That's the whole point of the arms business, isn't it? The risk is always someone else's. The courier, the recipient. The twelve-year-old conscript who catches the bullet you sold and dies in a ditch, screaming for his mother. It's a coward's business. I should have realised where you were headed years ago, got you thrown out of the Department before you made all these contacts and stole all that expert knowledge."

Mac nodded slowly. "And I," he said evenly, "should have pretended I never received that frantic call from a phone box outside Godensdorf, where you were standing half-drowned and bleeding like a stuck pig. I should have left you for the Stasi. But I didn't."

"I failed to do my duty, and you decided to do yours. And that makes us even?"

"I think it does."

The elevator doors swished open, revealing a stretch of anonymous grey corridor. Mac led him silently past a row of numbered doors, and shouldered open DOOR 47. Walls lined with glass cabinets glittered before them, displaying regiments of test-tubes and vials. Temperature and humidity indicators flickered, triggering tiny adjustments inside these sealed worlds.

"As you so rightly observed," Mac muttered, selecting a secure transport container from the only open shelves in the room, "there must be serious money involved."

"Chemical weapons."

"In these quantities? Peanuts." Mac scooped up another container, tossed it him. He caught it automatically, let it fall at his feet. "Don't display your ignorance, Tom."

"Biological, then."

Already busy with the lock on the first case, Mac grunted assent.

Drawing the semi from his pocket, Tom thumbed the safety off and pointed it at the cabinet in front of him.

Mac could see his reflection in the glass; clearly enough to understand, to stop picking the lock and murmur, "If I'd known you were suicidal, I'd have left you in the parking area."

"Step away from the cabinet."

"And then?"

"We go downstairs, load the trucks with conventional weapons, and leave. No one ever has to know this happened."

"No one has to know you got the better of me, you mean."

Tom shrugged.

"Much as I enjoy seeing you sweat, I think it's time I let you in on a little secret."

"Step away from the — "

"As in the rest of your life, Tom, old friend: you're firing blanks."

Swinging the muzzle a fraction of an inch to the left, Tom squeezed the trigger.

Mac hit the cabinet hard. The glass shivered, cracks radiating behind him like a halo. An internal alarm began to mewl frantically.

Pressing one hand to his stomach, where the impact had exposed the mesh of his kevlar vest, Mac whispered, "That little bitch . . ."

It all fell into place then. Her competence, her abrupt swings from hostility to subtle comfort. Her accent, her presence here at all. The hardest thing was believing that Mac had fallen for her in the first place, and he was still struggling to fit that piece into the puzzle when Mac bounded forward and hit him full in the chest.

The impact carried him across the width of the corridor; instinct warned him to drop his head forward a fraction of a second before he hit the wall, avoiding concussion. Pain flowered in his shoulders, spread down his lower back like the hands of a lover. Like Lucy's hands, moving over Mac, marking him for betrayal.

In the instant they were face to face, still, drawing breath for the renewal of hostilities, he whispered, "I'm sorry."

Then Mac's hand closed over his throat, fumbling for a pressure point on the artery to render him unconscious for restraint and a slow death, and he moved.

Boot in the groin: more kevlar, useless against a blunt impact. Mac's body bucked, his grip slipping, and Tom spun sideways, putting the wall to his left rather than his back. Dropped flat, jolting his opponent forward. Forcing him to use one hand to support his own weight. All textbook, all things Mac knew, but he was soft from a decade of signing deals and he couldn't get his balance back in time. A fist in the kidneys, a sideways twist, and they were rolling apart.

Black smudges blurred his vision, his legs seemed too weak to obey the urgent internal voice yelling at him to get up. When he finally made it upright, Mac was crouched in the doorway of the bio-weapons room, scooping up Tom's gun.

"I don't suppose the bitch put anything live in mine," he observed, swinging the semi to the horizontal. "Never mind. This will do — "

Muzzle flash. Sound. A split-second stretching to eternity.

No impact.

"Bitch," Mac said again, shaking the gun as if that would somehow changes blanks to live ammo. "The little — "

Two days of running, a cracked rib in Slovakia and an inventory of bruises gained in Hamburg, hours cramped in dirty trains or pacing railway stations, too scared to rest. Soft as Mac was, Tom wouldn't be able to take him in a fair fight, not today.

Turning without looking first, knowing there'd be only empty corridor and locked doors, Tom bolted for the elevators.

The sound of a shot followed him — sound and no impact, Mac checking it hadn't just been a random blank in the semi, damn his efficiency — and then, the footsteps.

He wouldn't make the elevators, not in a straight corridor. He needed to slow the pace, find cover, turn Mac from a running predator to a stalking one.

DOOR 33. DOOR 32.

STAIRWELL.

Shoving the door open, Tom lurched through. Safety railing to his left, the stairs plunging away into gloom. He didn't have the strength to vault the railing;

went over headfirst instead, fighting the impulse to grab at the metal, forcing himself to accept the fall, straighten up and get his feet under him before —

It hurt like nothing he'd ever known. It hurt so badly that for a moment, he was back in that fourth-floor cell, crying and sobbing and wishing he had the breath left to give them what they wanted, ready to betray but too far gone to manage it.

His legs weren't responding. Automatically, his hand moved to his calves, and stopped there, puzzled to find scar tissue under his jeans instead of raw and bleeding wounds.

Move, Whelan. Move or die.

His fingertips hooked over the threshold, dragging him forward, through the open exit door marked FLOOR FOUR.

"It was fated, wasn't it?"

The voice came and went. Sometimes it was Mac's, sometimes a familiar Stasi guard — the one with bad breath, or the sadist who always positioned himself where he had the best view of the 'interrogation'. Sometimes it was Lucy's voice, fragile with regret. The voice came and went, but the motion was real. Inch by inch, concentrating on the cold floor tiles, the occasional ridge of metal. The feel of the skirting boards as his shoe scraped against them for purchase. His dragging, useless leg, the wet knee of his jeans leaving long dark smears on the corridor floor.

Still running.

He had no idea where he was going, but, exactly like his life for the last twelve years, it was easier to keep running than to stop.

"Fated to end here," Mac explained, from some nebulous point in the darkness behind him. "Can you remember which cell was yours? It would add to the irony. Close the circle. It was your destiny to die here, Tom. Crippled and alone. You escaped it the first time, but you can't cheat fate forever."

Something in his hip pocket ground against the floor tiles as he hauled himself another painful inch forward. Without thinking, he reached for it.

The thin, brittle length of a meat skewer.

The corridor was in darkness; no way to tell where Mac was, if he was really still searching or just standing over his victim, spinning out the moment. Taking a chance, Tom felt his way to the skirting board and levered himself into a sitting position against the wall. Twisted at a new angle, his shattered knee protested; enough pain to clear his head, startle him back to a breathless alertness.

"I wonder," Mac said conversationally, fifteen or twenty yards off in the dark, "if the torture equipment is still down here?"

Grasping the skewer in his right hand, Tom drew a breath and held it.

He's tracking my breathing. Too dark to find me any other way. If he can't hear me breathing, then I'm still safely ahead of him somewhere, and he won't expect —

Something caught against his crippled leg, jolting a yell from him; but it was too late for warnings, Mac was already falling forward across this unseen obstruction, off balance and barely fast enough to break his fall with a hand. A soft grunt as the wind was forced out of him, and Tom's hand moved unerringly to the source of the sound, sliding up through Mac's hair to tangle into the top of the scalp. Left hand gripping, right hand stabbing in, cold metal into the softer bone at the back of the skull —

Liquid splashed into his face, blood or something worse; a convulsion tore Mac's body from his grasp, leaving gelled hairs between his fingers. Mac's legs landed across his lap, smashing against his ruined knee, and suddenly the corridor was red and black and lights danced in the distance . . .

By the time the lights stabilised, became the beams of searching torches and finally centred on his face, he was slumped on the cold floor beside Mac, resting against his shoulder like a lover, crying from the pain and a hundred other things he couldn't define.

"I should have given you more than one live round," Lucy's voice observed, as clinical as a teacher reviewing exam marks. "Doesn't look like you needed it, though. Maybe we should start issuing skewers as standard equipment, they certainly have their uses."

IN THE BACK OF THE MEDI-EVAC TRUCK — FRUIT LORRY OR SOME SUCH FROM THE outside, fully equipped ambulance within — Lucy sat down beside him and said, "I suppose you've worked it all out by now."

He looked past her; deliberately, leading her eyes to the headscarfed Turkish woman fighting the temperamental gears as they took another sharp country-road bend. "You set me up. The Slovaks, the ambush in Hamburg. All Departmental people. Scared me into going to Mac."

She bowed her head.

"Fuck you," he managed, closing his eyes to keep her sympathy at bay. "Fuck you all."

"In your position, I'd feel the same way. But we knew Mac was on the verge of a deal with someone big. Moving into bio-weapons. We fed him a line about there being impounded biological material stored here, and we handed him you. The only man he'd trust. And lo and behold, he calls his middleman over to help pick it up."

"Greenlea."

"Yup. And now we have Greenlea, scared to death and ready to sell out his own grandmother. Another operation, another step, and we pick up Mr Big in the US and we all get medals."

"And you. You're what, eighteen?"

"Twenty-two, actually."

"And you're going to get a medal and make a career and rise through the Department — "

She shook her head, jumping to the end of the story. "And end up like Mac."

"No. Like me." Tom smiled weakly up at her, knowing she wouldn't heed a word of it. "Killing men with meat skewers and not knowing the way out."

Lucy leant forward and kissed him lightly on the forehead. "If I find I need a way out, Mr Whelan . . ." He winced at the formality. "I'll come to you. You seem to be the expert on escaping things."

"We'll see," Tom murmured, visualising the look on Mayfield's face next time the Department offered its token annual round of voluntary redundancy opportunities. "We'll see."

crocodile lady
christopher fowler

Christopher Fowler has written nine
novels, including Roofworld, Spanky
and Psychoville, and seven collections
of short stories. His next novel is Get
Out of the House, his next collection
The Devil in Me, both due out in the
Spring of 2002. Chris runs Europe's
largest film and design agency in
Soho, and he lives in North London.
His novels are shifting into noir crime/
black comedy territory, but he still
loves horror stories and plans to do
plenty more of them.

1. FINCHLEY ROAD TO SWISS COTTAGE

London has the oldest underground railway system in the world. Construction began in 1863 and was completed in 1884. Much later it was electrified, and since then has been periodically modified. A great many of the original stations have been abandoned, renamed or resited. A partial list of these would include Aldwych, British Museum, Brompton Road, York Road, St Mary's, Down Street, Marlborough Road, South Kentish Town, King William Street, North End and City Road. In many cases the maroon-tiled ticket halls remain, and so do the railway platforms. Even now, some of these tunnels are adorned with faded wartime signs and posters. Crusted with dry melanic silt produced by decades of still air, the walls boom softly as trains pass in nearby tunnels, but the stations themselves no longer have access from the streets above, and are only visited by scuttling brown mice. If you look hard, though, you can glimpse the past. For example, the eerie green and cream platform of the old Mark Lane station can be spotted from passing trains to the immediate west of the present Tower Hill Station.

"You know what gets me through the day? Hatred. I hate the little bastards. Each and every one of them. Most of the time I wish they would all just disappear." Deborah fixed me with a cool eye. "Yeah, I know it's not the best attitude for a teacher to have, but when you know them as well as I do . . ."

"I think I do," I replied.

"Oh? I thought this work was new to you. Being your first day and all."

"Not new, no."

"My boyfriend just decided he wants us to have kids. He never liked them before. When he was made redundant he started picking me up from school in the afternoons, and saw them running around my legs in their boots and rainmacs asking endless questions, and suddenly he thought they were cute and wanted to have a baby, just when I was thinking of having my tubes tied. I don't want to bring my work home with me. We still haven't sorted it out. It's going to ruin our relationship. Hey, hey." Deborah broke off to shout at a boy who was trying to climb over the barrier. "Get back down there and wait for the man to open the gate." She turned back to me. "Christ, I could use a cigarette. Cover for me when we get there. I'll sneak a couple in while they're baiting the monkeys, that's what all the other teachers do."

Good teachers are like good nurses. They notice things ordinary people miss. Ask a nurse how much wine she has left in her glass and she'll be able to tell you the exact amount, because for her the measurement of liquids is a matter of occupational observation. The same with teachers. I can tell the age of any child to within six months because I've been around them so much. Then I got married, and I wasn't around them anymore.

But old habits die hard. You watch children constantly, even when you think you're not, and the reflex continues to operate even in civilian life. You bump into pupils in the supermarket. "Hello, Miss, we didn't know you ate food." They don't quite say that, but you know it's what they're thinking.

If there's one thing I know it's how children think. That was why I noticed there was something wrong at Baker Street. My senses had been caught off guard because of the tunnels. Actually, I sensed something even before then, as early as our arrival at Finchley Road tube station. I should have acted on my instincts then.

God knows, I was nervous enough to begin with. It was the first day of my first week back at work after twelve long years, and I hadn't expected to be have responsibility thrust at me like this, but the school was understaffed, teachers were off sick and the headmaster needed all the help he could get. The last time I had worked in the education system, the other teachers around me were of roughly the same age. Now I was old enough to be a mother to most of them, and a grandmother to their charges. I wouldn't have returned to Invicta Primary at all if my husband hadn't died. I wasn't surprised when the bank warned me that there would be no money. Peter wasn't exactly a rainy-day hoarder. I needed to earn, and have something to keep my mind occupied. Teaching was the only skill I was sure I still possessed.

Which was how I ended up shepherding twenty seven-to-eight-year-old boys and girls on a trip to the London Zoological Gardens, together with another teacher, Deborah, a girl with a tired young face and a hacking smoker's cough.

I hadn't been happy about handling the excursion on my first day back, especially when I heard that it involved going on the tube. I forced myself not to think about it. There were supposed to be three of us but the other teacher was off with flu, and delaying the trip meant dropping it from the term schedule altogether, so the headmaster had decreed that we should go ahead with the original plan. There was nothing unusual in this; the teaching shortage had reached its zenith and I'd been eagerly accepted back into the school where I'd worked before I was married. They put me on a refresher course, mostly to do with computer literacy, but the basic curriculum hadn't changed much. But things were very different from when I was a pupil myself. For a start, nobody walked to the school any more. Parents didn't think it was safe. I find parents exasperating — all teachers do. They're very protective about some things, and yet utterly blind to other, far more obvious problems. If they found out about the short-staffed outings, everybody would get it in the neck. The parents had been encouraged to vote against having their children driven around in a coach; it wasn't environmentally friendly. It didn't stop them from turning up at the school gates in people-carriers, though.

Outside the station the sky had lowered into muddy swirls of cloud, and it was starting to rain. Pupils are affected by the weather. They're always disruptive and excitable when it's windy. Rain makes them sluggish and inattentive. (In snow they go mad and you might as well close the school down.) You get an eye for the disruptives and outsiders, and I quickly spotted the ones in this group, straggling along at the rear of the tube station hall. In classrooms they sit at the back in the corners, especially on the left-hand side, the sneaky, quiet troublemakers. They feel safe because you tend to look to the centre of the class, so they think they're less visible. Kids who sit in the front row are either going to work very hard or fall in love with you. But the ones at the rear are the ones to watch, especially when you're turning back towards the blackboard.

There were four of them, a pair of hunched, whispering girls as close as Siamese twins, a cheeky ginger-haired noisebox with his hands in everything, and a skinny, melancholy little boy wearing his older brother's jacket. This last one had a shaved head, and the painful-looking nicks in it told me that his hair was cut at home to save money. He kept his shoulders hunched and his eyes on the ground at his feet, braced as though he was half-expecting something to fall on him. A pupil who hasn't done his homework will automatically look down at the desk when you ask the class a question about it, so that only the top of his head is visible (this being based on the 'if I can't see her, she can't see me' theory). If he is sitting in the back row, however, he will stare into your eyes with an earnest expression. This boy never looked up. Downcast eyes can hide a more personal guilt. Some children are born to be bullied. They seem marked for bad luck. Usually they have good reason to adopt such defensive body language. Contrary to what parents think, there's not a whole lot you can do about it.

"What's his name?" I asked.

"Oh that's Connor, he'll give you no trouble. Never says a word. I forget he's here sometimes." *I bet you do*, I thought. *You never notice him because he doesn't want you to.*

"Everybody hold up their right hand," I called. It's easier to count hands than heads when they're standing up, but still they'll try to trick you. Some kids will hold up both hands, others won't raise any. I had lowered my voice to speak to them; you have to speak an octave lower than your normal register if you want to impose discipline. Squeaky high voices, however loud, don't get results. They're a sign of weakness, indicating potential teacher hysteria. Children can scent deficiencies in teachers like sharks smell blood.

"Miss, I'm left handed." The ginger boy mimed limb-failure; I mentally transferred him from 'disruptive' to 'class clown'. They're exuberant but harmless, and usually sit in the middle of the back row.

"I want to see everybody's hand, now." *Sixteen*, and the four at the rear of the ticket hall. "Keep right under cover, out of the rain. You at the back, tuck in, let those people get past." *Seventeen*, the clown, *eighteen*, *nineteen*, the Siamese twins, *twenty*, the sad boy. "We're going to go through the barrier together in a group, so everybody stay very, very close." I noticed Deborah studying me as I marshalled the children. There was disapproval in her look. She appeared about to speak, then held herself in check. *I'm doing something wrong*, I thought, alarmed. But the entry gate was being opened by the station guard, and I had to push the sensation aside.

Getting our charges onto the escalator and making them stand on the right was an art in itself. Timson, the class clown, was determined to prove he could remount the stairs and keep pace with passengers travelling in the opposite direction. An astonishingly pretty black girl had decided to slide down on the rubber hand-rail.

"We step off at the end," I warned, "don't jump, that's how accidents happen." My voice had rediscovered its sharp old timbre, but now there was less confidence behind it. London had changed while I had been away, and was barely recognisable to me now. There were so many tourists. Even at half past ten on a wintry Monday morning, Finchley Road tube station was crowded with teenagers in wet nylon coats, hoods and backpacks, some old ladies on a shopping trip, some puzzled Japanese businessmen, a lost-looking man in an old-fashioned navy blue raincoat. Deborah exuded an air of weary lassitude that suggested she wouldn't be too bothered if the kids got carried down to the platform and were swept onto the rails like lemmings going over a cliff.

"Stay away from the edge," I called, stirring my arms at them. "Move back against the wall to let people past." I saw the irritation in commuters' faces as they eyed the bubbling, chattering queue. Londoners don't like children. "We're going to be getting on the next train, but we must wait until it has stopped and its doors are open before we move forward. I want you to form a crocodile."

The children looked up at me blankly. "A crocodile shape, two, two, two, two, all the way along," I explained, chopping in their direction with the edges of my palms.

Deborah gave me a wry smile. "I don't think anyone's ever told them to do that before," she explained.

"Then how do you get them to stay in lines?" I asked.

"Oh, we don't, they just surge around. They never do what they're told. You can't do anything with them. The trouble with children is they're not, are they? Not children. Just grabby little adults."

No, I thought, *you're so wrong*. But I elected not to speak. I looked back at the children gamely organising themselves into two wobbly columns. "They're not doing so badly."

Deborah wasn't interested. She turned away to watch the train arriving. "Crocodile, crocodile," the kids were chanting, making snappy-jawed movements to each other. The carriages of the train appeared to be already half-full. I had expected them to be almost empty. As the doors opened, we herded the children forward. I kept my eyes on the pairs at the back, feeding them in between my outstretched arms as though I was guiding unruly sheep into a pen. I tried not to think about the entrance to the tunnel, and the stifling, crushing darkness beyond it.

"Miss, Raj has fallen over." I looked down to find a minuscule Indian child bouncing up from his knees with a grin on his face. I noted that no damage had been done, then lifted his hands, scuffed them clean and wrapped them around the nearest carriage pole. "Hang on," I instructed as the doors closed.

"Miss, how many stops is it?" asked a little girl at my side.

"We go to Swiss Cottage, then St John's Wood, then Baker Street, then we change from the Jubilee line to the Bakerloo line and go one stop to Regent's Park."

"Miss, is there a real cottage in Swiss Cottage?"

"Miss, are we going to Switzerland?"

"Miss, can you ski in Swiss Cottage?"

"Miss, are we going skiing?"

"We're going skiing! We're going skiing!"

The train pulled away and everyone screamed. For a moment I sympathised with Deborah. I looked out of the window as the platform vanished. When I married Peter we moved out to Amersham, at the end of the Metropolitan line, and stopped coming into central London. Peter was a lecturer. I was due for promotion at the school. In time I could have become the headmistress, but Peter didn't want me to work and that was that, so I had to give up my job and keep house for him. A year later, I discovered that I couldn't have children. Suddenly I began to miss my classroom very badly.

"Miss, make him get off me." Timson was sitting on top of a girl who had grabbed a seat. Without thinking, I lifted him off by his jacket collar.

"I wouldn't do that if I were you," said Deborah. "They'll have you up before the Court of Human Rights for maltreatment. Best not to touch them at all." She swung to the other side of the central pole and leaned closer. "How long has it been since you last taught?"

"Twelve years."

"You've been away a long time." It sounded suspiciously like a criticism. "Well, we don't manhandle them anymore. EEC ruling." Deborah peered out of the window. "Swiss Cottage coming up, watch out."

2. SWISS COTTAGE TO ST JOHN'S WOOD

Many projects to build new tube lines were abandoned due to spiralling costs and sheer impracticability. An unfinished station tunnel at South Kensington served as a signalling school in the nineteen thirties, and was later equipped to record delayed-action bombs falling into the Thames which might damage the underwater tube tunnels. The Northern Heights project to extend the Northern Line to Alexandra Palace was halted by the Blitz. After this, the government built a number of deep-level air-raid shelters connected to existing tube stations, several of which were so far under-ground that they were leased after the war as secure archives. As late as the 1970s, many pedestrian tube subways still looked like passageways between bank vaults. Vast riveted doors could be used to seal off tunnels in the event of fire or flood. There was a subterranean acridity in the air. You saw the light rounding the dark bend ahead, heard the pinging of the albescent lines, perhaps glimpsed something long sealed away. Not all of the system has changed. Even now there are tunnels that lead nowhere, and platforms where only ghosts of the past wait for trains placed perma-nently out of service.

Trying to make sure that nobody got off when the doors opened would have been easier if the children had been wearing school uniforms, but their casual clothes blended into a morass of bright colours, and I had to rely on Deborah keeping the head-count from her side of the carriage. In my earlier days at Invicta the pupils wore regulation navy blue with a single yellow stripe, and the only symbol of non-conformity you saw — apart from the standard array of faddish haircuts — was the arrangement of their socks, pulled down or the wrong colour, small victories for little rebels.

I avoided thinking about the brick and soil pressing down on us, but was perspiring freely by now. I concentrated on the children, and had counted to fifteen when half a dozen jolly American matrons piled into the car, making it hard to finish the tally. I moved as many of the children as I could to one side, indicating that they should stay in crocodile formation. I instinctively knew that most of them were present, but I couldn't see the sad little boy. "Connor," I called, "Make yourself know please." An elliptical head popped out between two huge tourists. So unsmiling. I wondered if he had a nemesis, someone in the class who was making his life hell. Bullies are often small and aggressive because of their height. They go for the bigger, softer boys to enhance their reputation, and they're often popular with games teachers because of their bravado. There's not much I don't know about bullies. I was married to one for twelve years.

"I've got these new assignment books in my bag," said Deborah, relooping her hair through her scrunchie and checking her reflection in the glass. "Some government psychology group wants to test out a theory about how kids look at animals. More bloody paperwork. It's not rocket science, is it, the little sods just see it as a day off and a chance to piss about."

"You may be right," I admitted. "But children are shaped far more by their external environment than anyone cares to admit."

"How's that, then?"

"They recently carried out an experiment in a New York public school," I explained, "placing well-behaved kids and those with a history of disruption in two different teaching areas, one clean and bright, the other poorly lit and untidy. They found that children automatically misbehaved in surroundings of chaos — not just the troubled children but all of them, equally."

Deborah looked at me oddly, swaying with the movement of the train. Grey cables looped past the windows like stone garlands, or immense spiderwebs. "You don't miss much, don't you? Is that how you knew Connor was hiding behind those women?"

"No, that's just instinct. But I've been reading a bit about behavioural science. It's very interesting." I didn't tell her that before I was married I had been a teacher for nearly fourteen years. The only thing I didn't know about children was what it was like to have one.

"Well, I'm sorry, I know it's a vocation with some people, but not me. It's just a job. God, I'm dying for a fag." She hiked her bag further up her shoulder. "Didn't your old man want you to work, then?"

"Not really. But I would have come back earlier. Only . . ." I felt uncomfortable talking to this young woman in such a crowded place, knowing that I could be overheard.

"Only what?"

"After I'd been at home for a while, I found I had trouble going out."

"Agorophobia?"

"Not really. More like a loss of balance. A density of people. Disorienting architecture, shopping malls, exhibition halls, things like that."

"I thought you didn't look very comfortable back there on the platform. The tubes get so crowded now."

"With the tube it's different. It's not the crowds, it's the tunnels. The shapes they make. Circles. Spirals. The converging lines. Perhaps I've become allergic to buildings." Deborah wasn't listening, she was looking out of the window and unwrapping a piece of gum. Just as well, I thought. I didn't want her to get the impression that I wasn't up to the job. But I could feel the pressure in the air, the scented heat of the passengers, the proximity of the curving walls. An oversensitivity to public surroundings, that was what the doctor called it. I could tell what he was thinking, *oh god, another stir-crazy housewife.* He had started writing out a prescription while I was still telling him how I felt.

"We're coming into Baker Street. Christ, not again. There must have been delays earlier."

Through the windows I could see a solid wall of tourists waiting to board. We slowed to a halt and the doors opened.

3. Baker Street to Regent's Park

The world's first tube railway, the Tower Subway, was opened in 1870, and ran between the banks of the Thames. The car was only ten feet long and five feet wide, and had no windows. This claustrophobic steel cylinder was an early materialisation of a peculiar modern phenomenon; the idea that great discomfort could be endured for the purpose of efficiency, the desire to reach another place with greater speed. An appropriately satanic contraption for a nation of iron, steam and smoke.

"This is where we change," called Deborah. "Right, off, the lot of you."

"Can you see them all?" I asked.

"Are you kidding? I bet you there's something going on somewhere as well, all these people, some kind of festival." The adults on the platform were pushing their way into the carriage before we could alight. Suddenly we were being surrounded by red, white and green striped nylon backpacks. Everyone was speaking Italian. Some girls began shrieking with laughter and shoving against each other. Ignoring the building dizziness behind my eyes, I pushed back against the door, ushering children out, checking the interior of the carriage, trying to count heads.

"Deborah, keep them together on the platform, I'll see if there are any more." I could see she resented being told what to do, but she sullenly herded the class together. The guard looked out and closed the train doors, but I held mine back.

"How many?" I called.

"It's fine, they're all here. Come on, you'll get left behind."

I pushed my way through the children as Deborah started off toward the Bakerloo line. "You worry too much," she called over her shoulder. "I've done this trip loads of times, it's easy once you're used to it."

"Wait, I think we should do another head check — " But she had forged ahead with the children scudding around her, chattering, shouting, alert and alive to everything. I glanced back anxiously, trying to recall all of their faces.

I saw him then, but of course I didn't realise.

Four minutes before the next train calling at Regent's Park. I moved swiftly around them, corralling and counting. Deborah was bent over, listening to one of the girls. The twins were against the wall, searching for something in their bags. Timson, the class clown, was noisily jumping back and forth, violently swinging his arms. I couldn't find him. Couldn't find Connor. Perhaps he didn't want me to, like he didn't want Deborah to notice.

"Let's see you form a crocodile again," I said, keeping my voice low and calm.

"Miss, will we see crocodiles at the zoo?"

"Miss, are you the crocodile lady?"

Some of the children at the back moved forward, so I had to start the count over. I knew right then. *Nineteen.* One short. No Connor. "He's gone," I said. "He's gone."

"He can't have gone," said Deborah, shoving her hair out of her eyes. She was clearly exasperated with me now. "He tends to lag behind."

"I saw him on the train."

"You mean he didn't get off? You saw everyone off."

"I thought I did." It was getting difficult to keep the panic out of my voice. "There was — something odd."

"What are you talking about?" She turned around sharply. "*Who* is pulling my bag?" I saw that the children were listening to us. They miss very little, it's just that they often decide not to act on what they see or hear. I thought back, and recalled the old-fashioned navy blue raincoat. *An oversensitivity to everyday surroundings.* He had been following the children since Finchley Road. I had seen him in the crowd, standing slightly too close to them, listening to their laughter, watching out for the lonely ones, the quiet ones. Something had registered in me even then, but I had not acted upon my instincts. I tried to recall the interior of the carriage. Had he been on the train? I couldn't —

"He's probably not lost, just lagging behind."

"Then where is he?"

"We'll get him back, they don't go missing for long. I promise you, he'll turn up any second. It's quite impossible to lose a small child down here, unfortunately. Imagine if we did. We'd have a bugger of a job covering it up." Her throaty laugh turned into a cough. "Have to get all the kids to lie themselves blue in the face, pretend that none of us saw him come to school today."

"I'm going to look."

"Oh, for Christ's sake."

"Suppose something really has happened?"

"Well, what am I supposed to do?"

"Get the children onto the next train. I'll find Connor and bring him back. I'll meet you at the zoo. By the statue of Guy the gorilla."

"You can't just go off! You said yourself — "

"I have to, I know what to look for."

"We should go and tell the station guards, get someone in authority."

"There isn't time."

"This isn't your decision to make, you know."

"It's my responsibility."

"Why did you come back?"

Her question threw me for a second. "The children."

"This isn't your world now," she said furiously. "You had your turn. Couldn't you let someone else have theirs?"

"I was a damned good teacher." I studied her eyes, trying to see if she understood. "I didn't have my turn."

There was no more time to argue with her. I turned and pushed back through the passengers surging up from the platform. I caught the look of angry confusion on Deborah's face, as though this was something I had concocted to deliberately to wreck her schedule. Then I made my way back to the platform.

I was carrying a mobile phone, but down here, of course, it was useless. Connor was bright and suspicious; he wouldn't go quietly without a reason. I tried to imagine what I would do if I wanted to get a child that wasn't mine out of the station with the minimum of fuss. I'd keep him occupied, find a way to stop him from asking questions. Heavier crowds meant more policing, more station staff, but it would be safer to stay lost among so many warm bodies. He'd either try to leave the station at once, and run the risk of me persuading the guards to keep watch at the escalator exits, or he'd travel to another line and leave by a different station. Suddenly I knew what he intended to do — but not where he intended to do it.

4. King's Cross to Euston

There exists a strange photograph of Hammersmith Grove Road station taken four years after the service there ceased operation. It shows a curving platform of transverse wooden boards, and, facing each other, a pair of ornate deserted waiting rooms. The platform beyond this point fades away into the mist of a winter dusk. There is nothing human in the picture, no sign of life at all. It is as though the station existed at the edge of the world, or at the end of time.

I tried to remember what I had noticed about Connor. There are things you automatically know just by looking at your pupils. You can tell a lot from the bags they carry. Big sports holdalls mean messy work and disorganization; the kid is probably carrying his books around all the time instead of keeping them in his locker, either because he doesn't remember his timetable or because he is using the locker to store cigarettes and contraband. A smart briefcase usually indicates an anal pupil with fussy parents. Graffitti and stickers on a knapsack means that someone is trying to be a rebel. Connor had a cheap plastic bag, the kind they sell at high street stores running sales all year round.

I pushed on through the platforms, checking arrival times on the indicator boards, searching the blank faces of passengers, trying not to think about the penumbral tunnels beyond. For a moment I caught sight of the silver rails curving away to the platform's tiled maw, and a fresh wave of nausea overcame me. I forced myself to think about the children.

You can usually trace the person who has graffittied their desk because you have a ready-made sample of their handwriting, and most kids are lousy at disguising their identities. Wooden pencil-boxes get used by quiet creative types. Metal tins with cartoon characters are for extroverts. Children who use psychedelic holders covered in graffitti usually think they're streetwise, but they're not.

You always used to be able to tell the ones who smoked because blazers were made of a peculiar wool-blend that trapped the smell of cigarettes. Now everyone's different. Spots around a child's nose and mouth often indicate a glue-sniffer, but now so many have spots from bad diets, from stress, from neglect. Some children never —

He was standing just a few yards away.

The navy blue raincoat was gabardine, like a fifties schoolchild's regulation school coat, but in an adult size. Below this were black trousers with creases and turn-ups, freshly polished Oxford toecap shoes. His hair was slicked smartly back, trimmed in classic short-back-and-sides fashion by a traditional barber who had tapered the hair at the nape and used an open razor on the neck. You always notice the haircuts.

He was holding the boy's hand. He turned his head and looked through me, scanning the platform. The air caught in my lungs as he brought his focus back to me, and matched my features in his memory. His deep-set eyes were framed by rimless spectacles that removed any readable emotion from his face. He defiantly held my gaze. We stood frozen on the concourse staring at each other as the other passengers surged around us, and as Connor's head slowly turned to follow his new friend's sightline, I saw that this man was exhilarated by the capture of his quarry, just as I knew that his initial elation would turn by degrees to sadness and then to anger, as deep and dark as the tunnels themselves.

The tension between their hands grew tighter. He began to move away, pulling the boy. I looked for someone to call to, searching faces to find anyone who might help, but found indifference as powerful as any enemy. Dull eyes reflected the platform lights, slack flesh settled on heavy bodies, exuding sour breath, and suddenly man and boy were moving fast, and I was pushing my way through an army of statues as I tried to keep the pair of them in my sight.

I heard the train before I saw it arriving at the end of the pedestrian causeway between us, the billow of heavy air resonating in the tunnel like a depth charge. I felt the pressure change in my ears and saw them move more quickly now. For a moment I thought he was going to push the boy beneath the wheels, but I knew he had barely begun with Connor yet.

I caught the doors just as they closed. Connor and the man had made it to the next carriage, and were standing between teenaged tourists, only becoming visible as the tunnel curved and the carriage swung into view, briefly aligning the windows. We remained in stasis, quarry, hunter and pursuer, as the train thundered on. My heart tightened as the driver applied the brakes and we began to slow down. Ahead, the silver lines twisted sinuously toward King's Cross, and another wall of bodies flashed into view.

As the doors opened, fresh swells of passengers surged from carriage to platform and platform to carriage, shifting and churning so much that I was almost lifted from my feet. I kept my eyes focussed on the man and the boy even though it meant stumbling against the human tide. Still he did not run, but moved firmly forward in a brisk walk, never slowing or stopping to look back. The carriage speakers were still barking inanely about delays and escalators. I could find no voice of my own that would rise above them, no power that would impede their escape. Wherever they went, I could only follow.

5. Euston to Camden Town

Once, on the other side of that century of devastating change, Oscar Wilde could have taken the tube to West End. The underground was built before the invention of the telephone, before the invention of the fountain pen. Once, the platform walls were lined with advertisements for Bovril, Emu, Wrights Coal Tar Soap, for the Quantock Sanitary Laundry, Peckham, and the Blue Hall Cinema, Edgeware Road, for Virol, Camp Coffee and Lifebouy, for Foster Clark's Soups and Cream Custards, and East-man's Dyeing & Cleaning. These were replaced by pleas to Make Do And Mend, to remember that Loose Lips Sink Ships, that Walls Have Ears, that Coughs And Sneezes Spread Diseases. Urgent directional markers guided the way to bomb shelters, where huddled families and terrified eyes watched and flinched with each thunderous impact that shook and split the tiles above their heads.

On through the tunnels and passages, miles of stained cream tiles, over the bridges that linked the lines. I watched the navy blue raincoat shifting from side to side until I could see nothing else, my own fears forgotten, my fury less latent than his, building with the passing crush of lives. Onto another section of the Northern

Line, the so-called Misery Line, but now the battered decadence of its maroon rolling stock had been replaced with livery of dull grafitti-scrubbed silver, falsely modern, just ordinary. The maroon trains had matched the outside tiles of the stations, just as the traffic signs of London were once striped black and white. No such style left now, of course, just ugly-ordinary and invisible-ordinary. But he was not ordinary, he wanted something he could not have, something nobody was allowed to take. On through the gradually thinning populace to another standing train, this one waiting with its doors open. But they began to close as we reached them, and we barely made the jump, the three of us, before we were sealed inside.

What had he told the boy to make him believe? It did not matter what had been said, only that he had seen the child's weakness and known which role he had to play; anxious relative, urgent family friend, trusted guide, helpful teacher. To a child like Connor he could be anything as long as he reassured. Boys like Connor longed to reach up toward a strong clasping hand. They needed to believe.

Out onto the platform, weaving through the climbing passengers, across the concourse at Euston and back down where we had come from, toward another northbound train. We had been travelling on the Edgeware branch, but it wasn't where he wanted to go. Could he be anxious to catch a High Barnet train for some reason? By now I had deliberately passed several guards without calling out for help, because I felt sure they would only argue and question and hinder, and in the confusion to explain I would lose the boy forever. My decision was vindicated, because the seconds closed up on us as the High Barnet train slid into the station. By now I had gained pace enough to reach the same carriage, and I stood facing his back, no more than a dozen passengers away. And this time I was foolish enough to call out.

My breathless voice did not carry far. A few people turned to look at me with anxious curiosity. One girl appeared to be on the edge of offering her help, but the man I was pointing to had suddenly vanished from sight, and so had the boy, and suddenly I was just another crazy woman on the tube, screaming paranoia, accusing innocents.

At Camden Town the doors mercifully opened, releasing the nauseous crush that was closing in on me. I stuck out my head and checked along the platform, but they did not alight. I could not see them. What had happened? Could they have pushed through the connecting door and — God help the child — dropped down onto the track below? They had to be on board, and so I had to stay on. The doors closed once more and we pulled away again into the suffocating darkness.

6. KENTISH TOWN TO SOUTH KENTISH TOWN

The tunnels withstood the firestorms above. The tunnels protected. At the heart of the system was the Inner Circle, far from a circle in the Euclidian sense, instead an engineering marvel that navigated the damp earth and ferried its people through the sulphurous tunnels between iron cages, impervious to the world above, immune to harm. Appropriately, the great metal circles that protected workers as they hacked at the clay walls were known as shields. They protected then, and the strength of the system still protects. The tunnels still endure.

He had dropped down to his knees beside the boy, whispering his poisons. I had missed him between the bodies of standing, rocking travellers, but I was ready as the train slowed to a halt at Kentish Town. I was surprised to see that the platform there was completely deserted. Suddenly the landscape had cleared. As he led the boy out I could tell that Connor was now in distress, pulling against the hand that held him, but it was no good; his captor had strength and leverage. No more than five or six other passengers alighted. I called out, but my voice was lost beneath the rumble and squeal of rolling steel. There were no guards. Someone must see us on the closed circuit cameras, I thought, but how would eyes trained for rowdy teenaged gangs see danger here? There was just a child, a man, and a frightened middle-aged woman.

I glanced back at the platform exit as the train pulled out, wondering how I could stop him if he tried to push past. When I looked back, he and Connor had vanished. He was below on the line, helping the child down, and then they were running, stumbling into the entrance of the tunnel.

We were about to move beyond the boundaries of the city, into a territory of shadows and dreams. As I approached the entrance I saw the silver lines slithering away into amber gloom, then darkness, and a wave of apprehension flushed through me. By dangling my legs over the platform and carefully lowering myself, I managed to slide down into the dust-caked gully. I knew that the tall rail with the ceramic studs was live, and that I would have to stay at the outer edge. I was also sure that the tunnel would reveal alcoves for workers to stand in when trains passed by. In the depth of my fear I was colder and more logical than I had been for years. Perhaps by not calling to the guards, by revealing myself in pursuit, I had in some way brought us here, so that now I was the child's only hope.

The boy was pulling hard against his stiff-legged warden, shouting something upwards, but his voice was distorted by the curving tunnel walls. They slowed to a walk, and I followed. The man was carrying some kind of torch; he had been to this place before, and had prepared himself accordingly. My eyes followed the dipping beam until we reached a division in the tunnel wall. He veered off sharply and began to pick a path through what appeared to be a disused section of the line. Somewhere in the distance a train rattled and reverberated in its concrete causeway. My feet were hurting, and I had scraped the back of my leg on the edge of the platform. I could feel a thin hot trickle of blood behind my knee. The thick brown air smelled of dust and desiccation, like the old newspapers you find under floorboards. It pressed against my lungs, so that my breath could only be reached in shallow catches. Ahead, the torchbeam shifted and hopped. He had climbed a platform and pulled the boy up after him.

As I came closer, his beam illuminated a damaged soot-grey sign: SOUTH KENTISH TOWN. The station had been closed for almost eighty years. What remained had been preserved by the dry warm air. The platform walls were still lined to height of four feet with dark green tiles arranged in column patterns. Every movement Connor made could be heard clearly here. His shoes scuffed on the litter-strewn stone as he tried to yank his hand free. He made small mewling noises, like a hungry cat.

Suddenly the torch-beam illuminated a section of stairway tiled in cream and dark red. They turned into it. I stopped sharply and listened. He had stopped, too. I moved as quickly and and quietly as I could to the stairway entrance.

He was waiting for me at the foot of the stairs, his fingers glowing pink over the lens of the upright torch. Connor was by his side, pressed against the wall. It was then I realised that Connor usually wore glasses — you can usually tell the children who do. I imagined they would be like the ones worn by his captor. Because I was suddenly struck by how very alike they looked, as though the man was the boy seen some years later. I knew then that something terrible had happened here before and could so easily happen again, that this damaged creature meant harm because he had been harmed himself, because he was fighting to recapture something pure, and that he knew it could never again be. He wanted his schooldays back but the past was denied to him, and he thought he could recapture the sensations of childhood by taking someone else's.

I would not let the boy have it stolen from him. Innocence is not lost; it is taken.

"You can't have him," I said, keeping my voice as clear and rational as I could. I had always known how to keep my fear from showing. It is one of the first things you learn as a teacher. He did not move. One hand remained over the torch, the other over the boy's right hand.

"I know you were happy then. But you're not in class anymore." I raised my tone to a punitive level. "He's not in your year. You belong somewhere different."

"Whose teacher are you?" He cocked his head on one side to study me, uncurling his fingers from the torch. Light flooded the stairway.

"I might have been yours," I admitted.

He dropped the boy's hand, and Connor fell to the floor in surprise.

"The past is gone," I said quietly. "Lessons are over. I really think you should go now." For a moment the air was only disturbed by my uneven breath and the sound of water dripping somewhere far above.

He made a small sound, like the one Connor had made earlier, but deeper, more painful. As he approached me I forced myself to stand my ground. It was essential to maintain a sense of authority. I felt sure he was going to hit me, but instead he stopped and studied my face in the beam of the torch, trying to place my features. I have one of those faces; I could be anyone's teacher. Then he lurched out of the stairwell and stumbled away along the platform. With my heart hammering, I held Connor to me until the sound of the man was lost in the labrynth behind us.

"You're the Crocodile Lady," said Connor, looking up at me.

"I think I am," I agreed, wiping a smudge from his forehead.

Unable to face the tunnels again, I climbed the stairs with Connor until we reached a door, and I hammered on it until someone unlocked the damned thing. It was opened by a surprised Asian girl in a towel. We left the building via the basement of the Omega Sauna, Kentish Town Road, which still uses the station's old spiral staircase as part of its design. London has so many secrets.

The police think they know who he is now, but I'm not sure that they'll ever catch him. He's as lost to them as he is to everyone else. Despite his crimes — and they have uncovered quite a few — something inside me felt sorry for him, and sorry for the part he'd lost so violently that it had driven him to take the same from others. The hardest thing to learn is how to be strong.

Everyone calls me the Crocodile Lady.